Hot Tamara

Mary Castillo

AVON
TRADE

An Imprint of HarperCollinsPublishers

HarperCollins books may be purchased for education, business, or sales promotional use. For information please write: Special Markets Department, HarperCollins Publishers Inc., 10 East 53rd Street, New York, NY 10022.

FIRST EDITION

Designed by Elizabeth M. Glover

Library of Congress Cataloging-in-Publication Data

Castillo, Mary, 1974–
    Hot Tamara / by Mary Castillo.—1st ed.
        p. cm.
    ISBN 0-06-073989-4 (alk. paper)
    1. Mexican American women—Fiction. 2. Art galleries, Commercial—Employees—Fiction. 3. Mexican American artists—Fiction. 4. Los Angeles (Calif.)—Fiction. 5. Women immigrants—Fiction. 6. Fire fighters—Fiction. 7. First loves—Fiction.   I. Title.

PS3603.A876H67 2005
813'.6—dc22   2004052286

05 06 07 08 09 JTC/RRD 10 9 8 7 6 5 4 3 2 1

Hot Tamara

For my parents, Marti and Mike Castillo, who have been my biggest fans.

For Jen who has read the good, the bad, and the ugly, and still thinks I'm a good writer.

For Louise, Paula, and Dana, who have shared their talent and friendship.

For my editor, Selina McLemore, who fell in love with this book and made it even better.

And especially for my husband, Ryan, who was convinced that this would be the one.

This first book is for all of you.

June of last year

SHE WASN'T PREGNANT.

Thank God, she wasn't pregnant.

In the middle of her cousin Mireya's rehearsal barbecue, nature sent Tamara Contreras running into the bathroom and now the realization penetrated through the white-hot fear . . . *I'm not pregnant.*

Sitting in her Tía Yolanda's bathroom with goose-head faucets, antacid green walls, and pink towels with mermaids that looked like drag queens in shell bras, Tamara realized that she'd been freed.

Her cheeks and mouth jerked with the need to cry and laugh at the same time. Her breath came in shallow pants, her shoulders settled up past her ears, and her stomach braided itself tight.

Free. She was free like she'd just been behind the wheel of a spinning car with screaming tires throwing up smoke, the unstoppable centripetal force gluing her to the seat until suddenly it jarred to a stop, inches from the center divide. For five horrifying days Tamara sat in the spinning car, seeing all of her plans to hack off the apron strings flash before her eyes.

Good-bye ninetieth percentile score on the GRE. Good-bye Master of Fine Arts degree from the University of Southern California. Good-bye her own apartment in L.A.

And hello to little gold handcuffs that would bind her to Ruben Lopez forever.

If her mother knew . . . her eyes flew to the door. Tamara knew from twenty-six years of life that Mom had powers. Powers that saw through locked bathroom doors and carefully composed facial expressions. One hint of a clue that associated Tamara with pregna—

She covered her eyes with her hands, trying to shield herself from the weight of that word. If her mother linked the p-word and her daughter, Tamara would've wound up in Tía Josie's dress shop faster than a stick turning pink.

Now that all of her mother's friends' kids were married, Susanna Melendez Contreras, forty-nine, declared war against her daughter's decision to remain emancipated from the union. She deployed troops on all fronts, sent out the spies, then hunkered down in the foxholes, waiting for the perfect moment.

But Tamara was free. Fate had toyed with withholding the monthly bill, then went, *eh, we'll let you off this time.*

The bitch of it was that she couldn't even remember when she and Ruben had ever even hit the big one.

"Tamara! Tamara, what's wrong?" An iron fist rapped on the door.

Mom.

Tamara shot to her feet, then remembered she had locked the door. "I'll be right out," she called, putting herself back together. Thanking God again that packing tampons hadn't been just wishful thinking.

"Ay Díos, you had me so worried." A two-inch-thick door was apparently too much distance separating her from her firstborn child. "Let me in."

The last time Tamara checked, she was sure she'd been potty-trained at two. "I said I'd be right out."

"Are you sick? Was it the beans? I knew it. I told Yolanda she put in too much anchovy and . . ."

"Sorry, can't hear you!" Tamara twisted the tap on. God, cold water never felt so good. And the feel of those eye-singeing towels . . . she'd never take towels for granted ever again.

You just got a renewed lease on life, she told her pale reflection in the gilt-edged mirror. And as God as her witness, as God as her witness she'd never have unmemorable sex again!

"I'm fine," Tamara soothed, when she stepped out of the bathroom.

"Ruben and I were so worried, m'ija. You just ran off making a scene." Her mom's eyes widened, making her face into a perfect mask of maternal concern. "Everyone will think—"

Tamara tuned in the "mother filter" and dropped out. Remembering her Yoga class, she breathed while her mom continued with her lecture that Ruben had only been making a little fun of her when he said she never got to the point of her stories and . . .

Just two. More. Days.

Just two more days, and Mireya's stupid wedding would be over with, and she could finally—FINALLY—break up with *him*.

"Now, m'ija, it was just a little joke," her mom advised gently. But the hand that took her arm was anything but gentle as she led her down the hallway. "You know how our Ruben is."

Tamara caught that don't-get-angry look of hers when they walked into the living room, where Ruben waited with his arms crossed and his eyes focused on the ceiling. He hardly looked worried.

"Is she okay?" he asked, as if Tamara were deaf or two years old.

To the *ba-ba bum-bum-bum* rhythm of the ranchero music blasting from the backyard, Tamara retreated to her mental countdown: twenty-three hours, fifteen minutes, and eight seconds . . .

Ruben pounced on every opportunity to embarrass her in front of her family, her friends; it was like he was trying to mold her into something that would make their relationship *just right* instead of totally wrong.

"She's fine," Tamara snapped, when her mother opened her mouth to broker a peace treaty. She looked into his long-lashed brown eyes, which she once thought were the most soulful, loving she'd ever gazed into and smiled so hard she could've broken a tooth.

"Ay yi yi." Her mom looked down at the floor, resigned to a life of having to explain her daughter. *"La va a pesar."*

"I know," Ruben sighed. *"No le veo la punta."*

Goddammit. Tamara clenched her fist. They always did

that . . . spoke Spanish when they didn't want her to understand exactly what they were saying.

It was her Nana Rosa's fault.

Her chain-smoking, much-divorced Nana Rosa who insisted from her easy chair when Tamara's family visited on Sundays, holidays, and birthdays that the family was *New* Mexican. *No somos Mexicanos.*

You don't want them to be like those Mexicans who don't realize they're in America, her abuelita would advise Mom while her cigarette spit ash onto the urine yellow shag carpet. The woman probably had INS speed-dialed into her phone.

But that wasn't the point. Being unilingual was damn inconvenient when her parents, her aunts and uncles, their friends, and their friends' friends spoke Spanish. But her mother and her soon-to-be-ex-boyfriend? Now that was a damn shame.

Tamara resolved not to get mad. What was two more days compared to the ten years of being his girlfriend? She now had the rest of her life ahead of her.

"Babe, don't be that way," Ruben pleaded impatiently, when her gaze drifted longingly to the sliding glass doors.

"I have to find Isa," Tamara said, feeling as calm as Mother Teresa.

"Wait!" Her mom all but dived and wound her arms around Tamara's legs. If she had, she still would've managed not to spill her margarita. "Have you seen Carlos?"

Tamara nearly growled at the mention of her best friend's husband—associating him with that word was stretching it.

Now that she'd been given a second chance, Tamara replaced Carlos in the spinning car. Preferably with the air bag disengaged and a faulty seat belt.

The fantasy was probably a sin. "No. Why?" Still, it made her calm, as if fate had a plan that righted all wrongs.

"No one's seen him." Her mom's Tiffany chain bracelets slid down her arm when she smoothed a zealously manicured and moisturized hand over her carefully styled hair. "Has Isa told you anything?"

Tamara shook her head.

Isa really hadn't talked to her since . . . Tamara tried to think of exactly when they last had a real talk.

Her mom's eyes narrowed as if she didn't believe her. And then the strangest expression crossed her face.

"You know I really wished you hadn't cut your hair like that," she said. "It's so . . . *Tijuanera.*"

First, her mother drops a minor bomb that her best friend's husband was missing from his sister's wedding. Then she had to bring up Tamara's hair.

Wonder what she'd say when Tamara told her that at this time next year, she'd be finishing her first year of grad school and living in her own apartment?

Her mom pursed her lips, staring at Tamara as she most likely weighed the possibility that her real daughter had been misplaced at the hospital after delivery.

"I just wish you waited until after the wedding," she said, waiting for Tamara to take the bait.

"I like it like thi—"

"Ruben, be honest." Susan held her hand out, leveraging it at Tamara's head as if it were an abomination before all that was holy. "What do you think of this?"

If he hadn't been such a condescending ass, Tamara would've felt sorry for him being ensnared in the most dangerous of situations: bickering between a mother and her daughter.

"Mom, stop."

"What are you going to do when school starts again? You can't teach fourth-graders with hair like that. It won't grow out in time." Susan cocked her head to the side. "Well, maybe if we have it dyed. Hmmmm. I'll call Patty on Monday. Just one more thing on my list of things to do."

"No you won't."

Her mother arched a perfectly waxed brow. "¿Con permiso?"

When was she ever going to just let her be? Hadn't Tamara already done everything she'd wanted: homecoming queen, the steady boyfriend, and—God help her—the teaching position she sucked at?

"Now stop it, you two," Ruben drawled. "It'll grow out."

Tamara clamped her teeth together when she felt his hand sneak over her lower back. *Touch my ass, and I'll bite you.*

"But don't you agree, Ruben? Don't you think we need to do something about this?"

"It's different," he ventured diplomatically.

"You're no help," Susan said, convinced she'd won. "Ay, I need to go." She downed the last of her margarita and handed her glass to Tamara. "Yolanda and Josie are probably killing each other in the kitchen."

Tamara raised her eyebrows and fluttered her eyes when she read her mom's parting we'll-talk-later look.

Ruben stepped closer so someone could thread her way

toward the ever-grinding blender at the bar. "Are you over it, or do I have to wait till tomorrow when I can talk to you again?"

Two more days, Tamara reminded herself. "I'm fine."

Ruben didn't buy it. "I wasn't picking on you. I was just trying to point out—"

"Stop it, okay? I had to go to use the ladies' room, and I don't think I should have to explain myself." Good. She at least sounded calm. "Now I have things to do—"

"Like what? Try to keep everyone from looking down your dress?"

She felt herself go hot all over and not in the way a woman wanted a man to make her feel.

"Oh . . . is there something else you want to criticize?" she challenged.

"It's . . ." He paused with that *viejita* look on his face. "It's obvious that you're cold." He looked pointedly at her chest, then back up into her eyes, ready for her to explain herself.

She moved to cross her arms over her offending nipples, but stopped. *Wonder Woman wouldn't.* She planted fists on hips, slightly thrusting her chest forward.

"I'm just trying to help," he gently insisted. "You're going to start teaching full-time next year, and we agreed that you'd start wearing more mature clothes."

She agreed to a lot of things to shut him and her mother up. As badly as she wanted to, now wasn't the time to grind her new heels in his ears.

It would probably ruin the leather.

But Ruben liked to pick and pick at her until she exploded, so he could turn around and call her childish.

"I brought a sweater to wear when it gets cold," Tamara conceded, hating herself for backing down.

"Maybe you should put it on now," he said with that patient tone he liked to use when he felt she had finally seen his point of view.

She held her breath when he reached for her. Instead he tugged a piece of her hair. "Does that sweater have a hood?" he asked, thinking he was funny.

Desperate, Tamara retreated to her countdown, twenty-three hours, thirteen minutes. "I promised Isa I'd help her."

"Wait a second." He stepped closer. "Don't rush off in a tizz. Can't you stop being so sensitive?"

That did it. Smiling her big-party smile, Tamara finally took his advice and just got straight to the point.

"Fuck you, Ruben Lopez."

2

WILL BENAVIDES HELD his breath when he saw her. He stopped listening to his buddies shootin' the breeze. Hell, he just plain stopped when he saw Tamara Contreras for the first time in eleven years.

Goddamn. He took in the cute summer dress and long legs that looked even longer in the spiked sandals she wore.

Her smile hadn't changed. Her plump cheeks and round face were the same. But her hair had been long in high school. Long, straight, and dark. She now wore it all chopped and streaked, so it skimmed her jaw and made her look like a funky doll.

He went back to tearing the label off his beer bottle and pretending that he'd come just to catch up with his old high school pal Johnnie Muñoz, whose baby sister was finally marrying the father of her two kids.

Will hadn't seen Tamara since the day he graduated. She'd been selling refreshments at the snack stand under the bleachers. She'd smiled at him. But she could've been smiling at anyone. So he pretended that he hadn't seen her and walked across the field and two blocks away from the school to catch the bus home.

The sight of her now felt like a swift kick to the back of his knee.

Eleven years, he thought again, automatically laughing with the guys over a joke he hadn't heard.

Was she still dating that jerk-off, Ruben Lopez? Probably. Ruben was the kind of guy that cheerleaders and girls with smiles like Tamara dated. Not goateed, buzz-cut guys with callused hands like him.

Maybe if he was still in the Corps and showed up in his dress uniform, she might.

"So, Will, what the hell else you been up to man?" Johnnie tipped the neck of his beer bottle, then tossed his head back for a healthy swig.

"How come you been lyin' low?" asked Chuy, who was twenty pounds heavier than he had been in school.

Will cleared his throat. "Nothing exciting. Just working."

"So you're in the fire department, right? How come you got out of the Marines?" Johnnie asked.

"College, man."

"You went to college?" Johnnie couldn't seem to hold his head straight. "Where the hell'd you go?"

"Cal State L.A."

"Shit," Chuy mumbled.

"Man, you might want to tell people these things. How come you don't come by more often? I need you to touch up that tattoo you gave me in eleventh grade."

Will grinned, remembering how they cried like little

girls when he worked on their biceps. "I don't do that anymore."

"Why the fu—"

"Anyone want cake?"

Will tensed and, to the credit of his Marine training, he
didn't toss his bottle in the air. Calmly he looked up at
Tamara, who now stood within his arm's reach.

"Hey, Will," he heard Johnnie say. "You remember
Tamara, don't you?"

For a second Will imagined twisting Johnnie's head so
it faced backward. Once, only once, had he said anything
about how he lusted after this girl.

But Will played it cool and grinned at the girl he'd
never forgotten.

"Hi, Tamara. How've you been?" he asked. Oh yeah. He
was cool.

"Okay. Do you want some cake?" she asked, her lips
glossy in the stark lights that drowned the backyard John
Coltrane blue.

"This is the mystery man, Tamara," Johnnie said, taking
a piece of cake from her tray. "He's been in the Marines,
college. Now he's a fucking fireman." He turned to Will.
"Hell, are you married, too?"

"No."

"Gotta get you a family, dude. Best thing in the whole
world. Straightened me up. Did I tell you my Susie's expecting a boy?"

"You've been telling everyone," Tamara said, shifting
her tray uncomfortably. "Will, please take one. My arm is
going to fall off if I don't get rid of these things."

"Sure. Thanks." He carefully took one farthest from her

stomach, where the tray pressed up against her dress. Under a red sweater, it was white with little cherries.

His eyes strayed down to her toenails, painted pearly pink and delicate as teacups compared to his construction boots and jeans. He moved his foot under the table.

He looked back into her dark eyes, nearly forgetting his name.

"Are you still painting murals?" she asked with a faint smile.

"No. Are you?"

"Not anymore," she said, looking over her shoulder. "It's still there."

"That's good to know," he said, feeling Johnnie watching them.

"Yeah, well . . . nice seeing you again," she said as she walked away.

He needed another beer. The guys were too busy scarfing down cake to see his hand shiver as he reached for his fork.

Will had known she'd be here. But he had no fricking clue seeing her, talking to her would make him feel eighteen all over again.

"She and Ruben are next," Johnnie said, stuffing cake in his mouth. "Surprised they aren't married yet."

Careful to betray nothing, especially the sick feeling in his stomach, Will looked down at his cake. Shit. It was chocolate cake, with brown stuff in between the layers. He hated chocolate.

"Hell, with all these weddings and babies," Johnnie spoke through a mouthful of cake, "I'm gonna go broke, you know."

"Yeah, I guess," Will said.

Through the ringing in his ears Will heard Chuy start on about his pinche boss. He did his best to listen, but he kept imagining Tamara sitting there with him in her little white dress with red cherries.

Tamara cursed herself as a certifiable social retard.

Are you still painting murals?

There he was, in the flesh, and she yammered like a moron.

Obviously nothing changed. Will Benavides was still the unreadable, gorgeous guy that her mother would've put her in Catholic school to save her from.

Tamara never forgot the moment they met, and she shook his hand. It was like she *knew.* She could never put a specific word to what she knew and chalked it up to lust. Ever since, Will had a tendency to drift in and out of her fantasies—for the past ten or so years.

But now her in-flesh fantasy was here. All she had to do was look over her shoulder and—

"Hey, don't I get a piece?" Ruben asked behind her.

Startled, Tamara nearly dumped the last plate of cake onto the cement patio.

"Your fingers are cold," she protested, rubbing the back of her neck where he grabbed her.

"I've been trying to get your attention all night."

She clamped her mouth shut when he mashed his wet lips against hers. He smelled like beer and cigar smoke. She stepped back, resisting the urge to wipe her mouth.

"Why? To tell me I shouldn't use the f-word?" she spat.

"Do you have to be like that?" He stepped forward, and

she stepped back until she bumped against a pole supporting the patio overhang. "You look good, baby."

Tamara's skin flushed from her forehead to her feet as she saw people turn and smile at them. They were probably thinking, how sweet, how romantic.

Hey, folks, he's just drunk.

"Thanks," she said. "I uh . . . have more cake to pass out."

"It can wait."

"No it can't. Isa is waiting for me."

He reached for the tray. "I want to talk to you."

She tightened her grip too late. She realized he had her outnumbered when he handed it to his weasel man friend, Arturo, who materialized behind him.

"Knock it off. I want to go inside."

He rested his forehead on hers. "Be quiet a second while I figure out how to do this."

A splinter stabbed between her shoulder blades. Maybe she could duck down out of his arms and run for the safety of the kitchen.

Then she saw her mom standing next to Tía Yolanda; a glance over his left shoulder, and she saw her Tía Josie grinning broadly.

Oh, crap.

Her blood froze solid when she heard their prom song play over the crowd. Vanessa Williams's voice cooed about snow in June, suns and moons, about chances that had passed. They had been crowned prom king and queen to that song.

Her mind churned to keep up with what was happening. Her pulse choked off her air as Ruben unsteadily bent down on one knee. Someone sobbed. A woman. Probably her mom.

Ruben held on to her left hand with sweaty fingers. His eyes were dark with fear . . . and beer.

He swayed then caught his balance.

"Tamara," he said, projecting his voice over the crowd.

Tía Yolanda sobbed, "Oh Susan."

"Tamara, will you marry me?" he asked.

As if her neck was controlled by rusty hinges, Tamara slowly looked up from his pale face to the crowd. No one moved. No one spoke. They all wore smiles that were ready to burst into shouts of congratulations.

She was going to be sick.

What was the matter with him? Did he just decide at the last minute to ask her in front of all these people with no ring?

She had more cake to pass out.

She had to go to the bathroom.

She had to get the hell out of here.

But he waited on bent knee with her hand in his.

She couldn't say no in front of all these people. Not before Mireya's wedding.

But how fair would it be to him if she said yes when she didn't love him anymore?

Ruben's grip tightened on her hand.

She had to say something. Now. Five seconds ago.

Tamara's lips trembled as she parted them to speak.

Couldn't God just be God and give her a good old-fashioned earthquake that would send everyone running for their lives?

She opened her mouth, and all that came out was a puff of her breath hitting the cold night air.

The song droned on. Out of the corner of her eye, family and friends she'd known her whole life shifted awkwardly.

"I," she started, her voice ringing out. "I think we . . . no thank you, I don't think I—"

She looked up at her mom. Seeing the look of horror dawn on her face, Tamara wished she could've just played along and said yes.

"I have to go to the bathroom," she said, then turned and ran.

3

TWO HOURS, THIRTEEN MINUTES, and God only knew how many seconds Tamara had left until Mireya's wedding reception ended.

Stuck on the *Queen Mary*, a 1930s ocean liner converted into a hotel and permanently docked in Long Beach Harbor, Tamara had plenty of places to hide. But no place did the job like the ladies' room. Outside in the Grand Salon, three hundred people laughed, drank, and danced, except for the three waiting to kill her.

The door opened, and her best friend Isa's head peeked through. "There you are."

"I'm the last person you want to be seen with," Tamara said.

"That makes two of us." Isa's smile promised death as she shut the door behind her. "Carlos didn't show up."

"Never?" She took the glass of champagne Isa held out to her.

"Nope."

"Any idea where he is?"

Isa's jaw tightened, and that said it all. Carlos had been caught more than once with other girls ever since Isa became his prey when they were sixteen. Tamara had no idea what the guy did, but whatever it was kept her friend by his side.

"Wanna hide in here?" Tamara jerked her head back to the red and gold sanctuary of the ladies' room.

"For only a few minutes. I have to go check on Andrew before he decides to jump into the harbor."

They slumped on velvet-upholstered stools in front of sepia-toned, gilt-framed mirrors.

"You want to tell me what happened last night?" Isa asked.

With a sigh, Tamara pulled the ridiculously thin wrap around her shoulders, remembering the serrated looks and the pursed lips that had been aimed at her all day. "I couldn't say yes."

Isa folded her hands in her lap, knowing Tamara hated long silences.

"I mean, maybe I should've said yes so um . . . it wouldn't look so bad when Ruben and I had to walk down the aisle today but—" *But what?* She winced as the champagne sparked over her tongue. "I couldn't. I don't love him anymore."

Isa took her turn to sigh, deflating into the folds of her dress. She grabbed Tamara's hand and held on tight.

"What about your plans?" Isa asked. As the only person who knew about Tamara's plans, Isa leaned over to make sure they were alone. "You know, about USC?"

Tamara hoped she'd find out soon. If her application to USC came through, she'd have a perfectly good reason to move out of her parents' house. And not endure her mother's painful sighs, which said, *we were so close.* And not see Ruben at the very least until Thanksgiving or Christmas. And finally to be on her own. No longer to have to explain where she'd been or with whom. Complete adult freedom.

"I don't know yet." One more squeeze, and Tamara let go so she could stand up, reach under the lace-and-satin skirt of her ludicrous bridesmaid dress, and scratch the back of her thigh. Not only was the damn thing itchy, it was tighter on a no-chocolate, bloated day. "What?"

"I can't get used to your hair."

"Did you talk to my mother?"

Isa smiled, tugging her bodice up over breasts Tamara would've killed to have. "I like it. I just can't get used to it."

"Stop that." Tamara slapped Isa's hand from stuffing herself deeper into her dress. "Mireya paid good money for hers."

"You know I don't like these . . . things."

They'd been having this conversation since Isa literally burst into puberty in third grade. Tamara envied her big boobs, blue eyes, soft widow's peak, and proud Mexican profile. Isa'd been trying to hide ever since.

"Love them," Tamara said, downing the rest of the champagne. "What are you going to do about Carlos? Other than hide from his mother?"

Isa slanted a dirty look at her. "Don't change the subject." That was the problem with best friends. They knew all your dirty tricks.

"Seriously. Yolanda's gotta be tearing her hair out by now."

"He'll tell her some big story that somehow makes me at fault, and she'll believe him." Tamara saw through the nonchalant shrug. Carlos was once the man of Isa's dreams; but after she married him, she realized he and his mother were living nightmares.

Before Tamara could gently segue into the millionth conversation where she asked why Isa just didn't leave him, someone rapped on the bathroom door.

Their gazes swung to the door.

"You get it," Tamara said, after the second knock.

"Hell no, it's probably my mother-in-law."

"She wouldn't knock. Neither would my mother. It's probably Ruben." Tamara's voice hitched another octave on his name, and she wondered frantically where she could hide.

"Then talk to him," Isa pleaded. "You could work things out."

"I don't want to work things out with him—"

Isa slipped away before Tamara could tackle her to the floor.

"No!"

The traitor yanked the door open anyway. Shit. Okay. This was it. Tamara steeled her shoulders. The Time to Talk. The moment when Ruben noticed she'd been drinking in the ladies' room.

"Is she in there?"

Tamara's shoulders slumped with relief. Her seventeen-year-old brother's face smirked at her from the doorway.

"What are you doing skulking outside the girls' room?" she asked accusingly.

"Why are you and Isa trying to get drunk?"

Isa smacked his arm.

"Ow!" The big baby rubbed his arm.

Tamara and Isa exchanged a look that silently pondered how they could carry him outside and throw him over the side.

"I need to find my son," Isa said, pushing her way past Memo, who nursed his arm.

"Well, what do you want?" Tamara demanded, walking to the door.

He might have been a six-foot-two-inch baby, but he looked good in the sage-colored suit and red tie. She'd helped him pick it.

"We have to talk. Come on," Memo said, holding the door open for her.

She yanked up her wrap and stepped out into the foyer leading to the salon.

It was a beautiful room, she thought wistfully. The thirty-foot art deco walls gleamed like molded chocolate and the sepia-toned mirrors once reflected the faces of movie stars mingling with the rest of the first-class passengers over champagne and cocktails while an orchestra played under the silver-nickel bas-relief.

She frowned at the vulgarity of dancers bopping to the Chicken Dance.

"Come on." He took her arm. "You can walk, can't you?"

"Shut up."

"Come with me."

She sucked in her breath when the night air stabbed through the thin wrap. Memo led her away from the ballroom, down the stairs, to the second-level deck. The city

~~~~~~

lights of downtown Long Beach winked over the inky waters of the bay.

"Did you know that dress looks like a lampshade?"

She looked down at the stiff lace A-line dress with its gathered, itchy bodice. "I didn't pick it out. So what's going on?"

"I brought you something." He reached into his coat pocket and pulled out an envelope folded in half.

Suspicious, she looked at it, then back up at him. "What?"

"It's for you, from USC."

Tamara snatched it from his fingers. Her hands quivered, and her stomach coiled with anticipation. Three months of waiting would end after she opened it.

Wait a minute.

"How did you know?"

With a lift of his shoulder, he leaned sideways on the rail, trying to strike a pose that would make Cary Grant envious. Cary had nothing to worry about.

"I know things."

"Did Mom and Dad see it?"

"Nope."

"You didn't say anything to them?"

"Nope."

Tamara paused, weighing all of his possible motives. When he was born he had been the enemy. And then when he was six, Tamara couldn't help but take pity on him and beat up his tormentors. Finally, when he reached thirteen, they became allies. Now, as much of a sneak and a big baby as he was, they were friends.

But still, she had to ask, "How much will it cost me?"

"If I get accepted to Arizona State next year, will you tell Mom and Dad?"

"You applied to Arizona State?"

He lifted one shoulder. "Yeah."

"But I thought they said no."

"They told you no to USC."

She shook her head and grinned at him, proud he had the courage to go behind their backs at his age. But as his older sister, who'd walked the gauntlet more times than he, she had to be honest with him.

"They're not going to like it," she warned.

"But maybe they'll be so mad at you and won't care what I do."

He had a point, dammit.

They'd said no the instant USC came out of her mouth when she was seventeen. *A girl like you has no business in a dangerous city like L.A.*, her dad had said; the old words still scraped even now. Hell, they barely allowed her to attend USD and she only got to go because it was a Catholic school, her mother's ex-sister-in-law lived down the street, and Isa was going, too.

"I can't guarantee anything, especially if they're not talking to me," she said. "Then again, you're a guy. They'll probably let you go."

"Sucks for you, huh?" He stuffed his hands in his pockets. "Well, dude. Open it."

She rubbed her thumb over the USC logo. "I don't know," she murmured. "What if I didn't get in?"

He made a p-ish sound as he leaned both arms on the railing.

"You got in," he said with a careless shrug. "I saw your GRE scores."

She opened her mouth to ask how he had seen her GRE scores but didn't. She held the big payoff to a year of silence and painstaking planning in her hands.

"How about I open it by myself, then I find you later?"

He took in a deep breath and pushed himself off the railing. "Fine. I'll be inside."

Tamara faced the black rippling waters of the harbor, refolding the letter in case anyone saw her. She waited until his footsteps faded, then looked over her shoulder to make sure he was gone.

She ran-walked all the way to the lower deck at the stern of the ship. She wanted to laugh, she wanted to cry, wanted to shout all at the same time.

Don't be a basket case, she told herself as she sat down on a lone bench that faced a stretch of the southern coastline.

The sound of the ripping paper, the unfolding of the letter seemed to pound at her ears.

The letter shivered as she read it the first time, then the second time. It took the third time for her to realize . . .

. . . they rejected her.

The USC School of Letters, Arts, and Sciences Master of Fine Arts and Museum Studies program rejected her.

Just like that, her life hit the wall and burned. The late nights studying for the GRE, the secret trips to L.A. for the interviews, the foreign language test . . . All while suffering through those awful mornings when her hands cramped and her stomach twisted itself inside out as she drove to school with her mom.

She felt she'd earned herself a good cry, so she did, not caring what her mom or Isa or anyone would think when she walked back into that reception with raccoon eyes.

She sniffled and smelled cologne.

That sneaky punk followed her, she thought, when she heard the tapping of his shoes.

He cleared his throat, and asked, "Are you okay?"

He, who was now sitting next to her, wasn't Memo.

Holding her breath, she looked through watery eyes at Will.

"Oh God," she said, wiping her cheeks. "I'm sorry. I . . ."

"Tough night?"

She nodded, trying to smile.

"Anything I can do?"

She dared to look back at him, the tears welling up again. He frowned at his big hands folded in his lap.

"Well, maybe it's for the best," he said. "You pretty much said you didn't want to marry him last night."

A laugh shot out of her before her hand clamped over her mouth. She silently prayed to die.

"Sorry. I think I might have had too much to drink and . . ." Why was she telling him this? She held up the letter crumpled in her death grip. "This isn't about Ruben. I got rejected by USC."

He blinked. "That sucks. What did you apply for?"

She waited for the quirked lips and the elevator eyes that she was used to getting from guys. But Will didn't look like he was laughing at her. His light brown eyes were gentle as if—dare she even think it?—he actually cared.

That wasn't something she'd ever think Will Benavides

would do for anyone. Probably kick someone's ass, grind their face into the floor, or rip their arm off and beat them with it . . . but not sit there and care about *her*.

"My master's in fine art and museum studies," she answered, choking up again.

His eyes remained steadily locked with hers. "Can I read it?"

She shrugged, why not, as she wiped her cheeks with the end of her wrap. He took the letter and flattened it on his thigh.

Tamara was upset, but not enough to miss her opportunity to check out Will. In her memory, he seemed taller. But he was about five-ten like her dad. It was his broad shoulders and the bulldog way he carried himself that made him seem bigger.

He had a small forehead that was already lined from his default frown. His mouth was wide, and when he smiled, he was drop-dead handsome.

"It says that you were in the top tier of students," he said, pointing to the letter.

Caught staring, Tamara straightened in her seat. "I know."

"Don't you think you should try again?"

"Maybe."

When he studied her again, she realized his eyes weren't brown. They were hazel. With big inky black eyelashes around them.

"Do you want me to go back inside and never breathe a word to anyone that I found you out here as long as I live?" he asked, a grin sneaking across his lips.

"Yes. I mean no." She sighed, trying to keep the stiff

black lace and nude satin skirt from poofing up. "Don't worry. I won't jump. It's embarrassing enough to be seen in this thing alive."

He laughed softly. "It's not that bad."

"It's ridiculous."

"So why 'SC?" he asked.

She steeled herself against another shiver. "My dad used to take us up there for the games. He's kind of a workaholic, but he always had time to take us to the games. Sometimes we'd go early and walk around campus. He always said how if he had had the money, he would've gone to school there. He's a mechanic, but what he really wanted to do when he was a kid was go to law school, but—"

Dammit, she was babbling again. Her mom and Ruben always pointed out that she lost people's attention when she babbled.

"Will he be disappointed when you tell him?" Will asked.

"Tell him what?"

His eyebrow arched. "That you didn't get accepted."

"He doesn't . . . actually know. No one does. Except you, my brother, and Isa."

Before Will could ask more, it just poured clean out of her.

"My parents wouldn't let me go to USC when I was a freshman because they said I had no business being in such a dangerous neighborhood. Now they want me to get married and go back to this teaching job my mom set up that I really don't want. So last year I had enough saved to pay for some of the tuition and . . ." She stopped. "You probably don't want to hear any of this."

But Will did. He knew virtually nothing about her.

He sat back, hitching one arm over the back of the bench. Watching her as the water lapped against the ship and a breeze teased her hair.

"Not that I mind telling you," she said. When she brushed his sleeve, he felt the touch down to the bone. "It's just that we hardly know each other."

"I don't mind listening." He cleared his throat, watching her small hand fall back into the folds of that odd-looking lace dress.

"So, what exactly is"—he glanced back at the letter—"an art history and museum studies degree?"

"I would've picked a specific period in art to study and at the same time curated an exhibit for the university." He caught on to the way her spine straightened and her voice lost that hesitance. "I want to be a gallery owner."

He looked down at the streak of green paint on the inside of his wrist that he had missed when he washed up for the wedding earlier in the afternoon. Never in a million years would he have believed he and Tamara Contreras shared something in common.

"Eventually I'd like to own my own gallery, but . . ." She shrugged, then looked back out over the water.

"But what?"

"It's not a very practical idea."

"Ideas aren't supposed to be practical."

She smiled, but the corners of her lips quivered, and her eyes watered.

"Tamara, this isn't the end of the world." Instinctively he started to reach for her hand but held back.

"I know," she said, her voice wavering.

"I got turned down by three fire departments before I got hired by L.A."

She wiped the corner of her eye with her finger. Her other hand stayed nestled in her dress.

Don't do it, Will said to himself.

But hell. He held his breath when his dry, callused hand made contact with hers.

Her chin trembled.

"It's not like you have anything else to lose." He winced after he said it, but she laughed.

"You must think I'm a total loser," she managed.

"No I don't."

She grinned, shaking her head. "If I were you, I would think I was a loser."

He wiped a tear off her cheek with his thumb, feeling like his ribs would split open from the pounding of his heart. He'd never been this close to her. Sure as hell never held her hand, much less touched her soft face.

The only other time he'd touched her was that day back in high school when she shook his hand. She'd talked to him like she didn't know, like everyone else did, that he lived in a foster home and his mom was a drug addict and his dad was doing thirty at San Quentin.

He needed to get back into the reception, where Johnnie was trying to hook him up with some of his wife's single friends. The longer he sat with Tamara, the harder it would be to walk away.

But before he could move, she looked him right in the eyes and kissed him.

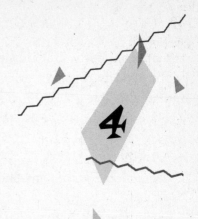

4

"OH MY GOD, you didn't!"

Isa stood wide-eyed on the other side of her dining room table, crowded with laundry. "You *kissed* him?"

"I did," Tamara said.

"Let me get this straight." She set the hand towel she'd been folding on the table. "You kissed Will Benavides?"

"I didn't mean for it to happen but he was there and he was being so sweet and I just—"

Tamara stared down at her twisted pile of towels, searching for the reasoning, the logic behind what was easily the dumbest-assed thing she'd ever done.

"What did he do?" Isa asked, pushing her wet hair out of her face.

Tamara never should've come over to Isa's house. But her inner Catholic girl burned for confession. And needed to forget that taste of him.

And after that long, awful wedding day, she couldn't chance getting cornered by her mother.

"Well . . ." The words packed themselves up tight in her

throat. Her body still burned after what happened last night. And part of her grieved she'd probably never see him again. "He . . . uh . . . he kissed me back."

She immediately began folding. Maybe Isa would let it go.

"And?"

Tamara tried the one-shoulder shrug. "I kissed him back."

Isa huffed. "Where were you when this happened? Did he say anything?"

Tamara thought back to last night and told herself, she was just going to give the bare facts. But then she opened her mouth, and every aching detail made Isa's eyes grow wider and wider until she finally sat down.

"Is this okay?" Will asked, his warm hand hesitantly settled on her thigh.

When she didn't answer—couldn't answer—he didn't make another move.

Instead he pressed his lips against her neck, tickling the side of her face with his hair.

Suddenly it wasn't that cold anymore. And her real-life kiss with Will was better than any of her teenage fantasies.

Will's lips were soft and warm. Not like Tamara thought he'd be. She tasted beer and him and with each inhale smelled that clean, almost grassy, cologne he wore.

Gently he parted his lips, invited her in. Tamara hesitated, but then he caught her face in his hands and drew her bottom lip into his mouth.

This was bad. This would send her to Hell.

But she didn't stop. How could she when his tongue gently played with hers?

She clutched at his jacket, holding on for dear life.

And that wasn't his belt buckle. Hell, that was *him*.

She made some helpless noise against his shoulder as his other hand found her hip, and he pressed her harder against him, rocking her into a mind-numbing rhythm that she couldn't get enough of.

He kissed her again while his blunt-tipped finger hooked under the border of her stockings.

And then footsteps tapped on the deck above them. People.

God, people!

Tamara pulled away, holding him at arm's length

Will's eyes were still closed. His eyelashes little fans over the delicate skin under his eyes and his big hand warm on her upper thigh.

She looked up and thank God, considering how many of her blood relatives were crawling all over the ship, no one found them. If it had been her mother, she wouldn't have just walked away. She would've jumped the railing and ripped them apart.

She looked back at Will, his eyes open and staring at her.

"I shouldn't have done that," were the first words out of her mouth.

"Oh God, Tamara. You didn't say that?"

Isa sat down, pressing her forehead with a linty dishrag.

"What else was I going to say?"

Isa smiled, clearly trying not to laugh. "That you've been in lust with him since you were fifteen?"

"Well, what was I—" Tamara blinked twice. "How did you know?"

Isa sent her a withering, how-stupid-do-you-think-I-am look.

"You don't think my mother knows, do you?"

The sliding screen door scraped open. "Can I watch TV?" Andrew shouted as if he were an eighty-year-old man.

Tamara wondered how his shirt managed to twist itself completely around his middle.

"Stay outside," Isa said.

"But I—"

"Outside. Your Tía Tamara and I are having adult talk."

He made eyes at Tamara, and her guilty heart jabbed her. *Sorry kid,* she said with a quirked mouth and a shrug.

"Go get yourself a Pepsi and play outside."

His eyes brightened, and his tennis shoes thundered over the linoleum to the refrigerator.

"Close the door all the way," Isa called over her shoulder.

"Thanks, Mama," he shouted, after slamming the refrigerator door and running back outside.

Tamara shut the screen door for him.

"So what did he say?" Isa paused. "You didn't sleep with him, did you?"

Will bent forward to take her mouth.

"Will, no wait!" Tamara nearly rolled off the bench, but somehow her feet hit the floor and she was standing.

The only thing that rooted her to the spot was the look on his face. She'd never forget his wide eyes and his parted lips, still wet from their kiss.

She took a step back.

"Hey, wait." He caught her wrist. His fingers were long enough to completely wrap around her wrist.

Some nameless emotion——frustration, dread, or loss—— balled in her chest and worked its way into her throat.

She wouldn't cry again. She could cry after she hid.

"I can't. I'm sorry," she heard herself giggling. "I don't know what I was thinking and . . . I need to go."

His grip tightened. "Come on. I'm not going to do any- thing," he said, with a tug on her arm.

You're not the one I'm worried about.

"You're going to trip head over ass in those shoes going up the stairs because you're crying again," he said sharply.

She tugged her hand back.

"You should go," she said. "I'm sorry, but I . . ."

Silently he stood up, staring at her as if she were some- one he couldn't figure out or even want to.

"I'm so sorry," she said, hysterical giggles bubbling up from the pit of her queasy stomach. "I don't know what's wrong with me. Please don't—"

"I won't tell Ruben," he interrupted, no emotion on his face. Holding out her wrinkled letter, he waited for her to take it back.

She wasn't going to tell him that; in fact, she really didn't care if Ruben found out. She just didn't want Will to think that she did this all the time. And if she'd been truly free, she wouldn't have stopped because she'd never been kissed like that.

But the explanation stayed, held in a headlock by her guilty conscience.

"You might want to clean your face up before you go

back," he said, in a voice that made her cringe, leaving the letter on the bench.

She bit down on her lip, nodding like a moron. But he had already turned away from her, his shoes snapping sharply against the deck as he walked away.

"So do you think I'm a"—remembering Andrew was somewhere outside, Tamara whispered—"a slut?"

"No. I mean . . . I wouldn't have done what you did because it's not like you've cleared things up with Ruben," Isa offered diplomatically.

She was a slut. Tamara hadn't officially broken up with him, and last night she was making out on a public bench for everyone to see. Except, thank God they hadn't.

"Tamara, don't. It's not like you're married or anything. It was a mistake."

She smiled back at Isa. It wasn't just any old mistake. It was an amazing—no!—horrible, terrible mistake.

She was the worst of women: the *cheating* slut.

"You're dying to know what happened next, aren't you?" Tamara asked.

"Yes, now stop feeling guilty and talk." She looked around Tamara to make sure Andrew was out of earshot. "The boy might come back, so hurry."

She took in a fortifying breath, then blubbered her lips. "I said I was sorry and he said he was sorry, then he left."

The refrigerator motor clicked on.

"He just walked away?" Isa asked.

Nodding, Tamara pulled a towel that had been twisted around another. Tears burned her throat, and she kept her eyes down so Isa wouldn't see the tears crowding at the rim of her eyes.

"And he said he was sorry?"

Tamara nodded, rubbing her nose, then doing a quick eye swipe.

She heard Isa sigh. They folded in silence. Tamara physically ached with guilt and this illogical sense of loss. That in one night she'd lost two things that had been cruelly dangled in her face, then yanked away.

Tamara wouldn't know how to explain it, even to her best friend with whom she'd survived honors algebra, virginity loss, unplanned pregnancy, and God help them both, a baby shower for Isa when she was pregnant after their freshman year in college.

"Now that the USC thing didn't work out, what are you going to do?" Isa asked.

The options weren't much. Stay at home with her parents, go back to a job she hated . . . face Ruben.

"I can't—" Her emotions caught up and snatched her voice. She heard Isa push her chair back and move toward her.

"This will stay between us."

And that only made it worse. She bit down on her lip, holding in the guilt and the loss when Isa's arms came around her. "Look at it this way, you got to kiss the guy you'd lusted over for years. Not too many women can claim they ever did that."

"I'm sorry." She sniffled and Isa handed her a towel with Sponge Bob smiling back at her. "Thanks."

"You're welcome. That must've been a hell of a kiss."

"Do you ever feel like you're not doing what you were meant to do?"

Something flickered over Isa's face, then it was replaced by an impenetrable stare.

"I don't have time for regrets."

"Don't you wish you could've gone to med school like you planned? By now you'd be starting your resi—"

"Internship." Isa backed away to her side of the towel mountain. "If I'd done all those things then, I wouldn't have Andrew. And I never regret him. Even when Yolanda reminds me how I ruined Carlos's chances at going to law school or that they had to buy this house for us so we'd have a place to raise our son."

Tamara knew better than to press. When Isa's lips got thin like they were now, she wouldn't budge, no matter what.

"So when are you going to talk to Ruben?" Isa asked primly.

"I don't know."

"Tamara, he's a good guy. Don't leave him waiting around for you to make up your mind."

Excuse me? She stared over the towel mountain, but Isa ignored her.

"He was drunk that night. If he really wanted to marry me, he would've asked my dad and proposed with a ring."

Isa ran her hand over a neat washcloth she'd squared. "He'll give you security. He'll never cheat on you or abandon you while he does God knows what." She carefully set the towel on the blue tower she'd made. "Trust me, when the lust wears off, that counts for a lot."

Maybe it did. But to Tamara, that just didn't count enough.

5

WHAT THE HELL just happened?

Will shut his eyes against the memory of Tamara straddling his lap, staring back at him in revulsion. He sat in his truck, the motor still running and the darkness surrounding him after pulling into the driveway of his house.

He'd considered going to a bar and finding someone to take home, but Will was a big enough boy to know better. So instead he blasted Guns N' Roses all the way home from Long Beach to get her out of his head.

But Tamara lingered, teasing him with that sweet paradise she'd nearly given him. And she haunted him with that look of realization of what she was doing and who with.

You are weak. You are pathetic. You are nothing.

The words of his drill sergeant echoed true once again. But Will had hoped that if he ever got one chance with Tamara, the last thing she'd look at him with was disgust. That she'd laugh at him.

Exhausted, Will hauled himself out of his truck and

walked across the yard to the apartment above his land-lady's garage. He thought about the sketches on his table, then remembered he had to be at work in four hours. The captain didn't have mercy for hungover, sexually frus-trated single guys.

He could've taken Tamara to one of the hotel rooms. He would've taken her with that dress bundled up around her waist, her back pressed against the door.

But honor and stupid pride had him dragging his sorry butt up to bed. Alone.

Stop thinking about her.

Forget her, forget that stupid kiss, and just . . . every-thing.

Will stopped midway up the stairs to his apartment over the garage when he heard Señora Allende's kitchen door click open.

He leaned back and saw a shaft of light stretch over the patio floor. He gripped the railing when a man backed down the stairs. But he stopped himself from tackling the creep when his seventy-six-year-old landlady walked into the doorway wearing her hair down and a fancy red silk robe.

What the—

"Now off with you," she hissed. "Go home, and I'll see you tomorrow."

The man Will struggled to identify mumbled some-thing. He craned his neck for another kiss, but she swatted him away. "*¡Basta!* Go home before someone sees you."

Will ducked his head back behind the garage. He heard the man walking down the path, whistling in the night. The gate hinges groaned and the latch snapped. Señora Allende shut her door. The yard went dark.

Will peeked around the corner of the garage, watching the man stroll down the middle of the street. The street-lamps cast pools of blue-white light on the chain-link fences and small gardens of the dark bungalows. In his suit and jauntily angled fedora, Señora Allende's boyfriend looked to be a very happy man.

So who is he, Will wondered, as a big smile stretched across his face. She obviously woke the man up after they—

Will's expression soured. He needed sleep.

"Yo, Willy!"

Will jerked to attention when Jones announced his name over the station P.A.

"You gotta visitor downstairs. Move it man."

Who the hell? For a moment Will didn't think he heard right. No one visited him here.

He looked back down at his mother's face, the way he'd seen her last, staring up at him from his sketchpad. He shoved it under his pillow, and his head wobbled when he stood off his rack. As soon as he got home to-morrow he was going to sleep.

With the dispatch dinging and squawking all night with med calls—thank God he was on the rig instead of the medic—he'd probably get up maybe three times instead of six.

Will's rubber-soled boots squeaked down the hall, past the TV room where the captain rocked back and forth in his easy chair, then past the gym room, where Eli the pro-bie played a racing game with the engineer on the hook and ladder.

"You're in trouble. Ohhh man! You are in big trouble,"

Jones said, when Will appeared at the top of the stairs. His shoulders were wide enough that they nearly brushed both walls.

"Shut up."

His lips spread into one big grin that promised hours of merciless teasing. "Go on, man. I wouldn't keep them waiting if I were you."

Jones backhanded Will's arm, snickering his way up the top of the stairs. With his fist Will pushed the door open into the barn, then grinned when he saw her. No. Them.

Señora Allende, his landlady and self-appointed abuelita, stood in front of the rig with her purse dangling from her arm. And next to her was Kirsten, in painted-on jeans, a tiny top that revealed a strip of tanned midriff and a vibe that shouted, MARRY ME.

He focused on Señora Allende, and her expression dared him to turn right back around and run. Kirsten was her comadre's—or one of them, at least—recently divorced granddaughter.

"I told you he was here," Señora Allende said to Kirsten, whose hair had been red the last time he saw her.

"Hi there," Kirsten purred.

God.

"Hey, ladies, this is a surprise," he said.

He smelled Señora Allende's gardenia perfume as he leaned forward to wrap her in a hug and plant a kiss on her powdery cheek.

Kirsten giggled when he hugged her, smelling like hairspray and mint gum.

"I wanted Kirsten to see where you worked. So she drove me down here after her Tía Rosalia's novena."

"Wow. Great."

"We brought you something," Kirsten gushed. She looked over at Señora Allende, and Will saw the flash of anger on her face. "Señora Allende," she said, her voice not so sweet. "Where are the cookies?"

"Ay, m'ija. I left them in the car. *Ay, mí memoria.*" She clucked her tongue, making a real production of it.

Will held his breath rather than roll his eyes.

"Oh, well, I'll get them," Kirsten said with just a touch of annoyance that aroused Will's protective streak.

"The door's over there, m'ija," Señora Allende directed.

Will released his breath, realizing how close he'd been trapped into the old, walk-me-out-to-my-car-alone trick.

Kirsten hesitated, but then her ass twitched its way to the door that led to the stairwell and out to the main exit.

When the door slammed, Señora Allende curled her crimson lips and smoothed a hand over her black hair with great satisfaction. Ever since Kirsten moved in with her grandmother a few months ago, she'd been making eyes at the both of them. Plotting and scheming.

"You baked cookies?" he asked, making his skepticism quite clear.

Even though she had grandkids from ages twenty-five to three, Señora Allende wasn't the kind of grandma who baked cookies and brownies. She was the kind who paid them to run down to the market for her lottery ticket, with some extra for candy.

"Not me," she said coyly. "Kirsten told me you've been too busy to take her out again."

Knowing it annoyed her, Will just stared silently.

"What?" Señora Allende asked. "She's single, she's Catholic, and she takes care of her abuelita."

Will got her a chair.

"*Ay que travieso.*" She sat in the chair he brought over. "There's always something wrong with them."

"So what? I'm picky." He grinned on the outside, but on the inside, he wasn't feeling so good.

She hissed disapprovingly, then shook her head. "She wants a home and a family, and I thought to myself, that's what my m'ijo needs. Not these . . ." She waved her hand around, thinking of something. "These *mujeres de la vida de alegres* you run around with."

"What?" He struggled not to laugh.

"You know what I mean."

Kirsten was exactly the kind of woman she called a . . . whatever she called them. He bet Kirsten never mentioned that she'd once invited him to spend the afternoon in her bedroom while Señora Allende and her comadres were at Thursday confession.

Of course, if she'd been Tamara, he would've run every step of the way to her bedroom and never left.

"M'ijo, I have something important to tell you," Señora Allende said, resting her hand on his knee. "I won't be around forever to take care of you."

Will looked up. He didn't like what he heard in her voice. "What's wrong?"

It was her turn to look down at the tips of her shoes. "I'm selling the house and moving to San Gabriel."

Her anguish sucked the breath out of him.

"I want to sell the house in the spring."

He could see that she'd planned to live out the rest of

her years in her little house with her old lady friends nearby and the church across the street. Not be passed around from her daughters' houses or sequestered in some guest room they cleared out to keep an eye on her.

"I also want you to work on the house for me," she said bravely. "And while you do that, why not get to know Kirsten better and get your pictures in one of those galleries."

"You don't—"

"No, no." She patted his knee, then brought it back to rest on her purse. "I spoke with Doña Villaseñor's nieta last night. The Jewish one." She dramatically rolled her eyes. "She has a gallery, and she needs artists."

"I told you I'm not ready to sell my"—he looked over at the stairwell door, then lowered his voice—"my paintings."

"¿Por que?" she asked, as if he had blasphemed in church. "Your pictures are beautiful, and they deserve to be seen." Her voice rang through the cement walls. "She's coming over next week, so have the best ones ready."

Will drew his hand over his chin. "I appreciate you talking to her, but I'm not—"

The doorbell buzzed, calling him to his doom.

"Let me do this," she insisted. The arrogance vanished, leaving behind an old woman who only wanted him to be happy.

"I want to see you with a wife who will give you a home and a family," she said, reminding him that it'd broken her heart when he told her about the apartments he'd lived in, then the foster homes. "You're a grown man, and it's time you stopped playing around and find the right girl."

Will had already found the right girl. She just didn't want him.

He slid off the bumper, making his way across the barn to let Kirsten in.

"Aquél que al ceilo escupe a su cara le cáe," Señora Allende called over from her seat.

He that spits up to the sky will get it on his face. Sighing, he knew he was about to step into the biggest pile of crap he could ever get into.

Kirsten was every single guy's wet dream, and when he woke up, his worst nightmare.

"Hi," she gushed, offering up the foil-covered plate in a way that nearly lifted her boobs out of her top.

"It was nice of you to bring Señora Allende by." If she heard the bladed edge to his voice, she didn't acknowledge it.

"Oh no problem. She mentioned it over lunch. She's such a sweetheart." She eyed him from head to toe like she had room enough to eat him.

Get rid of her. Don't get all annoyed. Just be nice but firm.

"Uh, thanks for the cookies," he said, taking the plate from her and backing into the station so she could pass.

She stopped within kissing distance of him, looking up through wispy bangs that had little pieces of blond in them.

He could've sworn her hair was red the last time.

"You're welcome," she said softly. "I missed you."

She locked her hands at the small of his back, and he checked to make sure Señora Allende wasn't spying.

Since she wasn't, it only meant she was really serious about seeing him hooked up with Kirsten.

"Hey, I'm duty—"

She brushed her lips against his and nipped his bottom lip. Her kiss was wet and hot. But it was like trying a different kind of food that was neither great nor terrible.

He'd already tasted great. When he didn't respond, her eyes fluttered open, then she rose on her tiptoes for more.

"Señora Allende's in there waiting."

"Just one more."

He released the door, and it slammed shut.

"I want to try a cookie."

Kirsten pouted, following him back into the barn, to safety.

Señora Allende smiled not with pride or satisfaction at a job well-done. She smiled at them as they walked toward her with hope that everything would be okay for him when she left.

Will's heart hurt. It really did. And it had never hurt for anyone except her and his brother.

So he thought as he got a chair for Kirsten and sat himself on the bumper of the rig. He'd do it. He'd take Kirsten out on a second date.

It wasn't like he had any other options at the moment.

6

"I TOLD YOU to turn down that TV," Susan hollered over her shoulder at John. "I want to talk to you before the girls come home."

"I know what you're doing," John said, from the brown recliner she threatened to toss out every winter. "Leave her alone."

Next time it wouldn't be a threat, Susan thought, aiming a deadly look she hoped he'd feel in the back of his head. She'd toss out that chair with him sitting in it.

"You're no help," she muttered.

"What?"

She shook her head, pushing up her bracelets so she could toss the salad. There were times when a mother had to confront her daughter.

It would hurt, and Tamara would get mad. Her tossing grew more frantic. But that was the price a mother paid when her baby strayed from the flock.

Susan had paid it before, and she'd pay it again.

But damn that *latoso*. He always stuck his damn head in the damn sand when things got ugly in the family.

"You're killing the salad."

He now stood on the other side of the breakfast counter, looking at her with the same eyes their children had.

"Aren't you worried that she hasn't come home straight after work ever since the wedding?" she demanded, not letting anything like his eyes or that distinguished gray at his temples throw her off topic.

"Yes. But she's an adult."

"Well I want to know. I'm her mother, and I don't like the way she treated Ruben the way she did."

He leaned both hands on the counter. "That's none of your business."

"Why am I the only one willing to talk to her? You were angry, too, after she made Ruben look like a fool in front of the whole—"

"Yes, but I was more mad at him because he didn't talk to me before asking her to marry him."

The man never had his priorities straight. "I thought you loved Ruben like a son."

"If Tamara doesn't want to marry him, then that's her choice."

He turned back toward the TV that he'd put on mute, and Susan indulged herself with the image of bopping him on the head with her salad tongs.

"So you're just going to let her mope around for a few more weeks?"

"She'll snap out of it," he said.

She curled her fingers into fists when he dug the remote out of his pocket and aimed it at the TV.

"Don't you dare."

He turned slowly, eyeing her like he was George Clooney. *"Le va a pesar, mujer,"* he warned. "You and your comadres are always meddling, and, just for once, you should let her figure it out on her own."

"I do not meddle." And that was the God's truth. She always let Tamara make her own decisions . . . after she guided her to them, of course. That's what mothers who loved their daughters did. And that was so much more than her mother, God rest her soul, had allowed.

After Tamara set a plate in front of her dad, her mom couldn't hold back.

"M'ija, have you talked to Ruben lately?" she asked in the same breath she asked Memo what he wanted to drink.

Nobody moved. Their eyes shifted, waiting for the other to speak first.

"Pepsi," Memo said.

"Since you're standing, get your brother some juice," Susan told Tamara.

"But I want a so—"

"Juice. You've had enough soda."

Tamara snatched the glass from a pouting Memo.

Thank God Isa agreed to Sunday dinner. Tamara had missed several Sunday dinners to avoid that very question: Ruben.

"John, do you want more gravy on your potatoes?" her mom asked.

"No."

"Are you sure? You hardly have any."

"I'm fine."

Tamara already had the pot in her hand when her mom said, "Honey, bring the gravy to the table."

Susan leaned toward Isa, sitting at the opposite end of the oak table that was reported to have traveled across the Atlantic with their Spanish ancestors. But when Tamara had looked, she saw the Sears Roebuck warranty tag stapled on the bottom. But she knew better than to open her mouth.

"Why is everyone so quiet?" Susan shook her head as she chewed.

Andrew giggled at something Memo did. Tamara eyed her dad, who chewed his food contentedly.

"Andrew, eat your carrots," Isa said. "Tía Susan made them for you."

He dug his fork into his mashed potatoes.

"Tamara, have you spo—" Susan persisted.

"Can we talk about something else?" her dad asked, attacking his chicken with his knife.

"But I'm just asking—"

"Mujer, I'm trying to eat."

Tamara exhaled, and her tongue floated down from the roof of her mouth. Isa and Memo were absorbed with their dinners.

Yes, she knew she had to talk about Ruben sooner or later, but . . . Sensing her fear, her mother went in for the kill.

"You know what I was thinking." Susan's voice seemed inordinately loud. "It would be an excellent idea for

Tamara to join the Principal's Advisory Committee next year? Don't you think so, Isa?"

Keeping her eyes on her plate, Tamara held all her frustrations inside.

"I don't . . . that depends on . . ." Isa started, her tone asking Tamara for help. "I guess."

"Mi vida," her dad said. "Pass me the vegetables."

Tamara chanced a look at Isa, who ignored her while her mom passed the bowl to her dad.

"Tamara, you should think about it," Susan continued. "It'll be good for your career."

Tamara slipped mashed potatoes into her mouth, rolling them around over her tongue, trying to swallow them. *Okay. Now is the time to tell her.*

"Tamara?" her mom asked. "You're very quiet tonight."

"I was—" She hesitated, locking eyes with Memo.

"What is wrong with you children?" Susan set her fork down, pressed her napkin against her lips, then folded her hands on the table. "What are all these looks about?"

They'd either gotten rusty, or her mom had their number all along.

"Nothing," Tamara said. The other two shoveled food in their mouths. God give her strength just to say that no, she wouldn't be on the advisory committee because she was taking a year off.

Who was she kidding? No one, not even Wonder Woman possessed the powers to say no to Susanna Contreras. Her mother had awards from just about every woman's and civic group and once had breakfast with the governor when she formed an outreach program to Spanish-speaking parents.

Just thinking the word "no" gave Tamara the shakes.

"I figured out what was wrong with that Supra today, Dad," Memo chimed in.

"Cracked rotors?" Her dad caught the ball and ran like hell.

"No there was—"

"Tamara, I'm waiting for you to answer my question," her mom insisted, cutting Memo off.

The ball simply disappeared, leaving her dad and Memo wondering what just happened.

Tamara stole precious seconds by wiping her mouth with her napkin and placing it ever so gently on her lap.

With one long breath she launched into the speech she'd practiced for a week. "I'm thinking that since I didn't do so well last year, and Principal Brand hasn't assigned a class to me, that I'd take a year off."

Tamara felt her mother's stare boring into the deepest corners of her heart.

"Are you finished, Memo?" her mom asked.

"Can I have—"

"Yes, and take it into the family room," her mom answered. "Andrew, go watch TV with Memo."

Tamara watched helplessly as Memo gave her a look that said, *I tried.*

"I should go and check on the . . ." Isa murmured.

"No, you sit," Susan commanded. "I want your help with this."

"Mom, I've put a lot of thought into this." She was already in the minefield, and there was no other way to go but straight ahead. "I have enough money saved—"

"To do what?"

For an uneasy second, while her stomach cramped, Tamara wondered if she could go on.

"Tamara, we've given you plenty of time to figure out what you want to do. We let you minor in art history so if you wanted to teach art, you would have that background. But the schools can't afford those programs, and we need good teachers. With time I know you'll grow into it, m'ija. We need young women like you and Isa to take up where my generation leaves off."

Tamara pressed back against the spindles of the chair, remembering her year of student teaching. Maybe not a complete disaster. But the countdown to the last day of school she'd tracked in her desk calendar probably wasn't a good sign.

"I don't have many years left, and I want to be here for you to guide your career, so you don't make the mistakes I made."

Her mom launched the heavy artillery: the next-generation speech coupled with the guilt.

"You don't need someone like me, Mom," Tamara said. "You need someone like Isa, who wants to be there."

Her mom's eyes widened, and her mouth dropped open. "Are you telling me that I put my professional reputation on the line for you—"

"Susan, *calmate*," her dad murmured.

"What for?" Her mom turned on him, talking as if Tamara were no longer there. "It's the same old problem *con tú hija* . . ."

Tamara rolled her eyes, not bothering to follow their conversation. If she'd stood up for herself in the very beginning, Tamara wouldn't be sitting here pretending to melt into the floor while her parents argued.

She was twenty-friggin'-six years old. Normal people her age didn't live at home with Mommy and Daddy. They rented tiny, over-priced apartments in bad or marginal neighborhoods with beer in the refrigerator and birth control pills or condoms out on the dresser because they had *lives*.

But here she was at home, serving her dad and brother and letting her mother "guide" her life.

She stood up.

"Excuse me, but where are you going?" her mom demanded.

"Tamara, park it," her dad warned.

Tamara hesitated, half-standing out of her chair. What would they do if she just left?

"Sit down," her mom ground out between clenched teeth. "We're not done with you."

So Tamara did what she always did; exactly what they told her.

"I cannot believe that after all this time you want to take *a year off*? You just got started. And the disrespect you just showed to me and your father . . . to teachers like Isa who worked hard to—"

"Mom—"

"I'm not done speaking." Her mother simply raised her voice over Tamara's. "Unless you plan on paying me and your father back for all the schooling we paid for; then you can take your year off. But with Memo going to college next year, we were counting on you to contribute to this household."

"What?" shot out of Tamara's mouth. "Why?"

Her parents shared a disbelieving look. "Until you are married you are part of this house and since you're finally working full-time, we need your help to put your brother through school."

"Let him get a job and loans like I did."

"This is different. He's going to business school, and he needs to focus on his studies."

Tamara could not believe what she was hearing. Since when did it suddenly become Albuquerque, 1903 again? Did she also have to do Memo's laundry when he came home on the weekends? Had her parents returned the few hundred cattle they'd planned to use for her dowry after she refused Ruben's proposal?

Her mother's voice pierced through the deafening frustration. "Your free ride is over. You have a responsibility to this family. Tomorrow you will go into Principal Brand's office—"

"She's in Europe till next week," Tamara said.

"Then you have time to realize that this idea of yours is—"

"No." The word hit the table like a bomb. "I'm taking a year off, and I'm using the money that I saved so I can get a job in an art gallery and my own apartment."

There. She said it. Why weren't there trumpets heralding her breakthrough? Where was the golden shaft of light spotlighting her for bravery?

Instead, her mother laughed. Laughed at her and once again she was twelve years old overhearing her mother say over the phone, "Isa's the daughter I'll never have."

Even though Tamara knew better, she really did wonder if they had been misplaced. Isa was quiet, smart, and already had a son, but ended up with parents who ignored her. Tamara was loud, a dreamer, who would probably give her parents cats as grandchildren.

"Ay, m'ija," her mom said, "you go ahead and think that. But we know you."

Isa moved a carrot across her plate.

"What do you mean by—" Tamara managed past her tightening throat. "You *know* me?"

Susan swallowed her drink and set it down with a click. "You were all high-and-mighty when we said no to the art degree. You said we could stop paying for your school, and you'd go part-time. But you thought about it, and you didn't go through with your threats." Susan picked up her fork and knife. "And this time, my dear, it won't be any different."

7

WON'T BE ANY DIFFERENT, HUH?

Tamara folded her arms, sitting back in a chair, in a gallery, in downtown L.A. on a day she'd taken off, without telling anyone, for an interview.

Well not this time. She'd spent the last two weeks shell-shocked that her mother laughed at her. Laughed at her. And then she got herself on the Internet and found this job. Now here she was. Waiting for the chance to change her life, grip her destiny by the neck and prove her mother wrong.

"Goddammit!"

Tamara looked up from her blank day-timer, startled by Nadine Frazier's ashtray-and-gravel voice booming across the gallery.

Jesse, who introduced himself as Nadine's assistant, grinned awkwardly across a desk made of honey-colored wood and topped by a sheet of smooth concrete. He delicately placed the cordless phone in its cradle as the small, pale woman dumped the contents of her bag on a desk while her voice mail blurted messages in the glass room behind him.

Even though Tamara might not work up the guts to come back, she leaned forward. "Should I reschedule?"

Jesse's neon blue eyes shifted from Nadine to her and back. "She'll be with you in a second." He shot up from his chair and walked into her office like something had flown up his butt.

"Nadine?" She overheard him through the glass wall. "Your eleven-thirty interview was here at eleven-fifteen. It's now a quarter to one."

Nadine held the bag over her head, then slammed it onto her desk. "Jesse," she yelled, her voice brittle to the point of breaking. "This is one of those days when one Valium won't be enough!"

Jesse's and Nadine's voices lowered to an angry hum. Tamara heard "I told you I can't do this anymore" followed by, "but you promised me." Out of the corner of her eye, Tamara saw flailing arms and hands gripping hair.

She turned to the window, staring out at the downtown buildings that lanced through a jaundiced summer sky. The gallery, housed in a converted cargo building along with an aikido studio and a café Jesse had told her was opening next week, stood right in the center of the burgeoning Santa Fe art colony east of Little Tokyo in downtown L.A.

Her options dwindled to two: take the teaching position and live at home forever, or step out into the world for the first time. But did she really think Nadine Frazier would be some Latina version of Mr. Miagi, who'd guide her, introduce her to the up-and-coming artists and collectors?

Nadine Frazier would probably eat her alive.

But visions of being teased and scorned as the family's fussy, hypochondriac old maid with a moustache like her Cousin Amy glued her to the seat.

The door clicked open, spilling Nadine's voice into the gallery.

"Tamara!"

She stood, not about to inform Nadine that her name was pronounced, Tah-Mar-Ah. Not Tamurah.

"Come in and have a seat."

She felt her inadequacies acutely as Jesse and Nadine watched her approach with her photocopied résumé, a scratched leather bag, and a rayon suit bought at a boutique next to the grocery store.

"Be nice," Jesse warned Nadine, who furiously stabbed the keypad of her cell phone with a brick-colored fingernail.

To Tamara, he assured, "I'll be right outside."

"Have a seat," Nadine muttered, gesturing with the phone to a couple of square chairs that faced what might have been a desk under the mess of paperwork. "I'll be just a second."

Nadine's office echoed the sleek yet warm wood tones of the gallery. A low bookshelf loaded to the groaning point sat against the wall. A series of framed Chinese symbols hung from silver wires on the exposed brick wall behind Nadine's desk.

"Sorry about that." Nadine plopped into a worn leather chair. She studied Tamara for a moment. "So what's your story?"

"Well after I saw your job posting and I found your *L.A. Times* article, I decided that I want to work in your art gallery." Tamara cleared her throat rather than visibly wince at the perkiness of her statement. "I worked at a children's museum for the last four years until last year, but I'm working there just for the summer. But before that I worked at the art gallery at USD, and I helped install the shows and with the catalogs—"

"I don't sell children's art." With that said, Nadine frowned down at a pink message slip.

Okay . . . now what? Should she wait until Nadine was finished reading whatever was written on the message?

"Go ahead," Nadine dared with a dry laugh. "You waited nearly two hours for this. Might as well make the trip worth it."

That sprang something lose inside Tamara. One moment she was uncertain and afraid; now she channeled her mother.

"If you're going to waste your time with me, why not leave your messages alone for a moment and hear what I have to say?"

Nadine's eyes flicked up, narrowing dangerously.

"I have a car, I can write, and I can answer phones," Tamara continued, figuring if she died at the hands of this woman, she'd go down with some pride. "I want to work as your assistant and help put together your next show. I'll work as many hours as you need me to work."

Her heart pounded as her mind caught up with what was spewing out of her mouth.

"I overheard Jesse say that he needs to talk to you about keeping the gallery open for some event in two weeks." She paused for breath. "I can be here in the evenings or on the weekends."

"Hold on. I have a feeling we're talking about two different things," Nadine said. "I thought you were here about the internship."

Internship?

"You're from USC, right? About the internship we posted at the art school?"

Tamara shook her head. "No. When I called to make the appointment I told Jesse I wanted to talk to you about the job on the Internet. But I'm applying to the museum studies program and figured that some practical experience might help my chances an—"

Nadine rubbed the skin between her eyebrows. "We're not hiring, and I don't foresee us hiring anytime in the near future."

Tamara's spine deflated as she mentally crossed another option off her list.

"But you won't get what you need with some intern," Jesse said, now standing in the doorway.

"Excuse me," Nadine exclaimed. "But this is my interview. And no one told you to post anything on the goddammed Internet."

"I told you I'm not doing this anymore, Nadine. I have my business to open, and you've sat on this long enough."

Tamara looked from him to Nadine and back.

"And I'm not coming back to save your ass if some cheap-assed intern doesn't work out." He wagged a threatening finger. "So do this right, and hire someone who'll do a decent job."

"I can't afford to pay someone full-time to answer phones and do the job I'd need her to do."

An exasperated sound exploded from his lips. "God, you sound like your mother."

Nadine gasped with absolute devastation.

"I have money saved." Tamara paused when two pairs of eyes shooting daggers at each other zeroed in on her. "Give me thirty days of part-time work—"

"I said I can't pay you."

"Bullshit," Jesse muttered.

"I know," Tamara said, recklessly. "But if I can prove myself and gallery sales can support a small salary, maybe you can hire me."

"Do you have gallery sales experience?"

"No."

Nadine looked like she was about to blast off her chair and into the open-beamed ceiling.

"She's willing to work for free, Nadine," Jesse said without drama. "After the upcoming show, you'll make enough to pay her something."

Nadine's lips puckered sourly. "You're making a lot of big promises. As far as I can see, you don't have the experience to back it up."

"Let's try it for a month," Tamara insisted.

Absolute silence reigned. She sensed Jesse willing Nadine to accept.

"Fine." Nadine sat back in her chair. "Okay let's do this. I'll pay you eight dollars an hour and free parking for thirty days. And Jesse can give you a job at the café next door for some extra cash." Nadine turned to him. "Right?"

"Of course," he said.

An invisible hand clutched the back of Tamara's neck and held on. She did it.

"And get this straight," Nadine spoke up. "I don't need someone who'll get her feelings hurt all the time. I'll ask you to do everything from handling clients to picking up my dry cleaning. Understand?"

"Completely," Tamara pledged, balling her sweaty hands into fists. She smiled but didn't get one in return.

She just stepped off a cliff even though she had no guarantee there'd be a safety net at the bottom.

But she didn't need a net. What she needed was an apartment.

"Jesus Christ, I hope Candace calls in sick Monday," Kirsten said, as Will pulled her chair back from the dinner table. "I swear if I have to hear one more time about her allergies, I'm going to kill her."

And if he had to hear one more complaint about her period, her coworkers, or another ex-boyfriend, Will would kill himself.

She kept on after she sat down, as he walked to his seat. Her litany of woe could probably be heard clear across the Stinking Rose from the velvet tent where they sat.

Seriously, though, what the hell was he supposed to do with this information? Solve her problems? Tell her everything was going to be okay?

After two dates since Señora Allende bombarded him with cookies, selling her house, and Kirsten, Will knew that all he had to do was nod every now and then so she'd think he was listening. Her voice receded to a frantic, annoying whine while her hands flailed about. Will's mind was left free to return to Tamara.

Why did he have to walk over to her that night of the wedding? Why did he stop to talk to her? Why did he kiss her back?

Didn't he realize back then that Tamara would ruin him for all women?

His blood turned cold at the thought.

"Maybe you should quit your job," he offered, when Kirsten took in a gulp of air.

"Excuse me?" She leaned forward, her low-cut blouse giving him a panoramic view he really didn't appreciate.

The waiter, thank God, arrived with menus. Will ordered a beer and she an iced tea after she piously announced she didn't drink alcohol.

"So you really think I should quit my job?" Kirsten paused, making that sassy head move. "Why the fuck would I do that?"

The woman sitting at the table next to them glanced over and then back at her plate when he caught her.

"You don't seem very happy there, so I thought maybe you'd be happy somewhere else," he said.

She looked at him like she just crapped her pants.

"So you're telling me that I complain too much?" she asked.

"No, of course not," Will answered, moving his water glass out of her reach. *Just get through this night,* he told himself, unpeeling his fingers from the fists they curled into. "You just don't seem to like your job, that's all."

"I *love* my job." She opened her mouth and eyes wide, in the way an opera singer does before letting the audience have it. "Look, if we're going to start seeing each other, I won't put up with this shit."

Out of the corner of his eye he saw the woman watching them again like they were a bad car accident.

"I don't let any man tell me what to do. Not after Tony, my husband of two years. He tried to control me to the point where I had to get a restraining order and . . ."

Señora Allende would think twice about eating one of Kirsten's chocolate chip cookies if she saw the psycho who made them.

How was he going to keep her from digging in her hooks permanently? Call him crazy, but he knew she was the kind that would start haunting the station, his apartment, or worse, Señora Allende's house.

"So do you know what you want to order?" he asked, desperate to end her ranting.

She smiled and made circles over the table with her fingertip. Will felt an eerie tickle along the back of his neck.

"You're really sweet, you know that?" she asked, all sugar and butter.

Will grinned, thinking of Señora Allende. Let this serve as a lesson never to let a seventy-six-year-old woman dictate his dating life.

"So," Kirsten cooed, scooting in her seat. "Did I tell you about my new church?"

Will had a feeling she was about to do so.

8

TAMARA CRANKED THE WHEEL of the ancient VW Karmann Ghia to turn onto her parents' street. Her heart thumped a little faster the closer she got.

Although daylight faded like a memory, kids on razors scooted under the dusty trees, shouting and laughing. The smell of barbecue drifted out from backyards, and Mrs. Cole in short shorts and a tank top watered her thirsty lawn.

She was really leaving all this. In just one day she had lassoed fate and come home with a closet-sized apartment and three thousand dollars in her wallet from the trade-in of her Honda Civic.

Just as her parents' house came into view, she downshifted and winced as the little car shuddered.

Biting on her bottom lip, she yanked the stick out of third and crammed it into second while pumping the clutch. The gears growled in agony, the car bucked three times, then it died.

She'd never been good at driving stick. But she'd get the hang of it.

And she'd always wanted a Karmann Ghia. It had been one more thing that had been deemed unsafe and unfit by her parents. So even if it did need a little fixing here and there, she got more money and the car she'd always wanted.

Who could argue against that logic?

"What is that?" her brother Memo yelled, holding a basketball under his arm.

The engine whined as she restarted it. Finally, it sprang to life like an oversized lawn mower.

"Shut up and get out of the way," she yelled, nearly drawing blood from her bottom lip as she concentrated on moving it out of first.

The car lurched forward, nearly giving her a heart attack as she saw the rear of Memo's VW Beetle come at her.

"Hey, that's my car!"

"I know, I know," she muttered, forcing the stick into reverse.

Tamara slowly backed the car until it stood parallel to the sidewalk. She switched off the engine, her ears buzzing after rattling in it for two hours.

She leaned over to pull her backpack off the passenger-side floor. When she sat back up, her parents and—oh God—Ruben materialized out of nowhere. Her mother clutched her chest with one hand and her dad's arm with the other.

"Where have you been?" she screeched. "We thought something happened that you were dying in the street!"

Braving the inevitable, Tamara heaved the door open and faced all of them on unsteady legs.

Don't let them smell fear, she thought, turning to smile at them over the roof of the car. This was her life, her car, and her decision. Well, at least it sounded good.

She cleared her throat. "So what do you think?"

Her dad tucked his chin down, a deep frown ridging his forehead as he walked alongside the car.

"I know it needs work," she started. A good offense was a good defense. "But with the trade-in, I got three thousand dollars in cash."

Her smile was lost on him as he studied the dent above the right rear tire.

"I don't even know where to start, Tamara."

"Where is *your* car," her mother demanded, leaving Ruben standing by himself.

"Why is the roof painted with primer?" Her dad stared at it with horror. "These tires are almost bald, and I can smell your brakes."

"I um . . . I have something to tell you," Tamara explained, looking to Memo for help. He made the sign of the cross.

"I should go," Ruben said.

"No, Ruben, you have to stay," her mom decided. "We need you to help us with this mess."

"What mess?" Tamara asked, knowing full well what mess her mother was referring to. "Ruben, please go."

"Don't you dare leave," Susan shouted. She turned to Tamara. "This is my home, and he's my guest. He stays."

"Susan," her dad warned. "Let him go home."

Tamara dared not speak, much less move. She'd only seen her dad contradict her mother once. Only once. She remembered how her dad begged for her mother to let him in the house afterward. Just like now, that one time had been because of her.

Her mother trembled with fury. "Are you pregnant?" she demanded.

Tamara's jaw unhinged.

"Hey, Dad," Memo interrupted. "I can do some of the repairs at the shop. Tamara can just pay me for the parts."

"Memo, go to your room," her dad said.

"Why should I go to my room? She brought home the junker, not me."

"Why would you even think I was—" Tamara tried to ask.

"What else would you need three thousand dollars for?" For a second, Tamara thought her mom was going to hit her. "Why would you do this without talking to your father?"

"For my apartment." Tamara swallowed. "I'm moving to L.A."

Her mom gasped.

"I got a part-time job in a gallery and needed extra money to rent an apartment."

Memo pivoted and hustled into the house.

"I submitted my resignation. I won't be coming back next year," she finished.

Her mom's hair flipped back and forth as she shook her head in denial. "We will clear up all of this mess first thing tomorrow. Your father will get your car back, and I will explain to Principal Brand that this was all some misunderstanding—"

"Will you just butt out?" Tamara was either going to cry or spontaneously combust from twenty-six years of being her control freak mother's daughter.

"I'm moving out, and I'm not coming back. You can laugh all you want, but this is my life, and I'm tired of letting you—" She couldn't speak, and tears turned the world to a gray, watery mass.

"Butt out?" her mom repeated. "When have you ever showed us that you're capable of making a mature decision?"

"Never," Tamara cried, making an absolute fool of herself instead of presenting her decisions like a mature adult. "You've never let me make any of my own decisions."

"How could you do this to our family?" Susan shouted for all the neighbors to hear. "It's bad enough you made a fool of poor Ruben in front of everyone we know. How am I going to face them . . . Principal Brand and my colleagues after they hear about this? Did you think for one second how this would affect everyone around you?"

Tamara wiped her eyes clear.

"Do you even care?" her mother asked.

Tamara slowly shook her head no. Not anymore. She'd been caring about what other people would say for too damn long.

Her mother stiffened, as if she'd just been slapped. "Okay, we'll see how this goes." Her eyes filled with tears and the corners of her mouth pulled down. "If you do this, Tamara, if you keep this car and take that ridiculous job in L.A., you are no longer part of this family. You only bring disrespect to your father and me."

Susan turned, thought about it, then turned back around. "Don't you have anything to say about this?" she demanded of John.

Oh no, thought Tamara. No one was going to talk about her like she wasn't there. Those days were over.

"If you have something you want to say," Tamara said, stepping in between her mom and dad, "then say it to me *in English.*"

A car passed behind her.

Her mother crossed her arms tight over her chest, walking straight over and putting her face in Tamara's.

"I don't know who you think you are, but you're not my daughter I raised to respect her parents and her *familía.*"

Tamara felt her hot breath against her face.

"You're so self-centered that you can't see how your idiotic decisions hurt everyone around you." Her mom's voice cracked. "We do these things for you because you can't. You're making a mistake, and as far as I'm concerned, I want nothing to do with it. You want to move to L.A.? Fine. Go. There's nothing for you here, and when you fall on your face, don't bother to come running to us."

Tamara stared down at her hands, which had fused themselves into a tight ball. The hurt pressed down on her chest, but she wouldn't cry. She wouldn't show how deeply her mother's words sliced.

Her mom's sandals clicked furiously as she walked away. She felt her dad come over, holding herself taut, fully expecting another attack.

"You always wanted one of those things," he said.

"I'll pay Memo to work on the car at the shop," Tamara promised. "I need to start my job in two weeks, so I'll just have him work on the important stuff like the brakes and the tires."

"Memo has more important things to do." He sighed. "We have customers, and we have to finish their work—"

He looked at her through tired, hooded eyes. "Tamara, I wish you hadn't done this."

"I'm sorry, Dad," she said, her throat tight. "But I have to."

She wished she could explain how right and at the same time, how terrifying it felt to take Nadine's offer. To finally take charge of her own destiny.

Even if the weight of it seemed unbearable.

"I hope you know what you're doing," he said.

She sniffled and tried to smile. *So do I.*

And then the last thing she needed happened. Ruben briefly touched her arm.

"Want to walk me to my car?" he asked.

She'd rather curl into a ball and chew her hair. But she owed him an explanation and had avoided it all this time. They walked side by side to his always washed and waxed 4-Runner parked two cars down.

"You okay?" he asked.

"Not really." She looked away to wipe away runaway tears with the heel of her hand.

"So what made you decide to move to L.A. all of a sudden?"

"Remember when I organized that art show in high school? You and Arturo built the walls."

"Yeah."

"Well, even though everyone fought me on it, said it was too much money and would take too much time—" She shook her head, remembering how her mother had been so proud when she saw what Tamara had done. "That's when I decided I wanted to have my own art gallery. Remember how I used to talk about moving to New York or L.A. or San Francisco?"

"We were kids, Tamara. What if this thing doesn't pan out? Don't you want to have a house someday and some security?"

"Look, I'm just trying to answer your question. I've wanted to move away from here ever since I was fifteen. But I always let my mom, you, and even Isa talk me into staying."

His shoes scraped against the pavement as he turned. "Are you saying this is my fault?"

He wasn't getting it. He never would get it.

Tamara made herself look up at a guy other women would mow her down to get next to. Well, they could have him. Ruben was probably the perfect guy for someone, but he wasn't the one for her.

"No. It's my fault," she said.

He scratched the back of his head. She knew he did that when she exasperated him. "Look, I know I should've called or something before I showed up here but I . . . I just want to know if this is really it between us?"

Tamara mentally sorted through all the stock lines to soften the truth.

But there were none. "I don't love you anymore."

He blinked. "How long haven't you loved me?"

The vise on her throat tightened. "I'm sorry, Ruben."

He laughed softly. "I don't know what I was thinking that night. I thought you were getting impatient about us not getting married, and that's why you were so unhappy."

Tamara forced herself to look at him. She was too tired, too numb to feel much of anything.

"Talk about not knowing what the hell was happening right in front of my face," he finished.

"Ruben, I don't know what to say other than I'm so sorry. I should've been more up front with you and—"

"With the next guy, try to be a little more truthful." Ruben stepped back, walking toward his car. "It's no fun being the party clown."

9

THE MORNING AFTER his date with Satan's ex-wife, Kirsten, Will walked into his studio, inordinately grateful for the little things in life that a man who had faced death could only appreciate.

He'd taken a shower the second after he got home. Even though that one kiss with Tamara put sex on his mind constantly, hugging Kirsten gave him an instant soft-on. So he washed away the hug he gave her, the kiss she gave him, and that nasty way she licked his neck. He even considered burning his clothes, but figured a wash and a spray of Lysol would do the trick.

As he turned to the large canvas resting on two easels, he felt himself seduced out of this reality and into the one he'd sketched on canvas. He took a pencil and, as always when he first approached a sketch, it roamed over the rough figures he'd blocked in: his mother, his brother Ricky, and himself.

Will's eyes traveled from his brother to the six-year-old boy he had once been. He could almost feel the stick in his hand that he swatted at some poor person's bush. His mother sat on the bench waiting for the bus with their bags at her feet. Ricky as always sat with her, keeping an eye out for the bus so they wouldn't miss it.

No matter how hard he had tried, he'd never forget that day. She'd woken up early and put cereal and orange juice out for them.

"I'm getting a job today," she said. "So hurry up and eat, so I can get to the interview on time."

But she hadn't looked at them when she said it. She just went into the bedroom he shared with Ricky and shut the door.

"Eat your cereal," Ricky said, pouring milk in his bowl.

"Where are we going?" Will asked.

"Don't know. But pack your colors and some small toys, okay?"

"Okay, but I still think we should . . ."

Knocking. Someone was knocking.

It occurred to him that people were outside his garage, knocking on his door.

He left the pencil on the counter and went to the door. The sun burned his eyes as part of him remained captured in that vivid somewhere of his past.

Señora Allende's gardenia perfume was the first thing he sensed.

"Hey, what's—"

She marched passed him. "Where are they?" she demanded.

"What?"

He felt a soft hand daintily pat his arm. Doña Villaseñor smiled sweetly up at him, her hair cut short and curled tight. She was one of Señora Allende's comadres from the church across the street.

"Good morning. *¿Como esta Usted?*" he inquired, always feeling awkward around delicate old ladies. Except Señora Allende. No one could call her delicate.

"*¿Buenos días?*" Doña Villaseñor laughed as if he made a joke. "Ay, m'ijo. You work too hard."

"I try to tell him, but he never listens to me," Señora Allende said in Spanish.

He felt someone walk past him. "Hi," she said, looking at him through thin blue-black sunglasses.

"Hi."

It took every cell of willpower Will had to keep from asking what the hell was going on. He was just getting to some good stuff when she marched her lady friend and this . . . this Flavor of the Week into his studio.

Did the old woman have no shame whatsoever about parading single women under his nose?

He studied her suspiciously. She left an invisible trail of cigarette smoke in her wake as she murmured to Doña Villaseñor. She kinda looked Mexican, small and thin——too thin for his liking——and wearing a dark, flowered dress with red flip-flops. Her black hair shot out in a riot of curls.

"Will," Señora Allende announced, pointing to the woman. "This is the woman I was telling you about. This is Doña Villaseñor's nieta."

He knew he was supposed to know her name, Will offered her his hand. "Will Benavides."

"Nadine Frazier," she said, gripping his hand like a man.

He looked at Señora Allende, hoping she'd end the suspense as to what they were doing in his studio at . . . Will realized he had no idea what time it was.

Doña Villaseñor rattled out in Spanish, "Matilda, tell him to bring out his paintings. She's very busy."

"What's going on?" he asked Señora Allende.

Her eyes rolled heavenward as if beseeching God himself for intervention. "Your paintings, m'ijo. For the show in November. Where are they?"

Then the lightbulb upstairs came on. Doña Villaseñor's granddaughter was the gallery owner. He didn't know if he should be embarrassed or thoroughly pissed off at having his work interrupted.

He turned his glare from Señora Allende to Nadine and back.

"Go look at his paintings," Doña Villaseñor hissed.

Nadine lowered her sunglasses so she could get a better look at him. Her abuela slapped her arm again.

"I own a gallery in downtown. Nana has been calling me nonstop for a month—

"*Tres meses*," Doña Villaseñor corrected.

Nadine glanced at her nana and stepped out of a swatting hand's reach. "So I thought while I was visiting her today, I'd see what you were all about."

Nice. She was here to make her grandma happy.

"I don't have anything that's finished," he said.

"What?" Señora Allende demanded indignantly. "Then show her the ones that are almost finished."

"Look if this is a bad time—" Nadine was cut off when Doña Villaseñor stepped forward.

"No. You came all this way. We want to see them."

God save him from old ladies, their granddaughters, and . . . and women in general.

If it hadn't been for the proud look on Señora Allende's face, Will would've turned on his heel and left. No one but Ricky and Señora Allende ever looked like they were proud of him, and for that he walked to the cupboard where he kept his paintings.

His hands trembled, and his heart did funny things in his chest. He doubted Nadine would come right out and tell him they sucked. Then again, a bland I'll-call-you-it-was-nice response would be even worse.

Señora Allende and Doña Villaseñor whispered behind him. Not arguing. Probably plotting, which from his experience carried greater consequences.

He carried two canvases, propping them up on the counter. A quick glance at Nadine studying his sketch on canvas sent cold panic straight through his heart.

"That's not done yet."

Nadine didn't seem to hear him. "Hey, can someone turn on more lights in here?"

"Will, open the doors," Señora Allende said, joining Nadine behind his canvas.

Unable to bear watching them study his work, Will pushed the doors open. When the heat of the late afternoon socked him, he realized how long he'd been sketching.

He turned, and Señora Allende stood right in his face.

"What is *she* doing in your painting?"

"Who?" he asked.

"*Tú madre.*" She said it as if the word tasted filthy. "That's her, isn't it? She doesn't deserve to be in one of your paintings, and I—"

"Hey, it's just a painting."

"Just a—" She breathed in, and she appeared to grow ten inches taller. "How can you say that?"

"Because it's just—" He lowered his voice. "It's not a big deal. I'm just getting it out of my head."

"That's the time, no?" she asked in Spanish. "The time she—"

"How long have you been painting?" Nadine called across the room.

"I . . ." He cleared his throat. "About four years."

"Where did you attend art school?"

"I didn't." He cleared his throat, pushing the memories of his mother and Ricky back where they belonged. "I just took a few classes at Cal State L.A."

Nadine frowned, then looked back at the little girl he painted walking through an empty lot in Watts. "How often do you paint?"

"Will paints every day he's not on duty," Señora Allende answered for him. "Sometimes I have to come in here and make him to go eat."

Nadine walked to the next canvas. "Why do all the subjects have their backs turned to us?"

Hell if he knew. But before Señora Allende piped in, he answered, "That was just the way I saw them."

"So what do you think, m'ija?" Doña Villaseñor asked, walking over to stand next to her. "Do you want them for your gallery?"

Will shifted his weight from one foot to the other then shoved a hand through his hair. His work in a gallery? Huh, he didn't think so.

He still held his breath, waiting for Nadine's answer.

"That depends," Nadine said casually. Her gaze made a bull's-eye with his. "Two paintings make a pretty small collection. I'll need eight pieces to start off with. I take it you haven't shown anywhere."

"Just at Cal State L.A." He crossed his arms over his chest. "I didn't sell any."

"Do you have a publisher?"

"No," he said, not quite sure what a publisher was.

Tapping her foot, she considered him.

"So what else do you have?"

10

July

SUSAN HAD TO get out of the house. She'd listened to Tamara pack up her bedroom for two weeks.

Her cup snapped on the counter. She didn't care that some of the tea sloshed over the sides. Its black acidity bit the back of her throat, much like the awareness that Tamara was leaving for a place that had no room for her mother.

"Are you okay?" John grumbled from his end of the counter.

"I'm fine."

"Are you going to say good-bye?"

She ripped a paper towel off the roll, attacked the spill, then the bottom of her cup.

"Susanna?" John only used her full name when he meant business.

"I have a lot to do for Josie's barbecue tonight."

He sighed, and the newspaper crumbled. "Come with us to her apartment. Just try—"

"What, John? Try what?" Her fist swallowed the paper towel.

"Try to make peace with Tamara before she leaves," he soothed. "Remember how you said you'd never do the same thing your mother did?"

Fury stiffened every muscle as she shook her head with disbelief. Now he wanted to talk about their daughter. *Now* he wanted to fix things. What had he called her when she tried to get him to help her talk to Tamara that night?

A meddler.

"She needs my meddling like she needs another hole in the head," she repeated through her teeth.

"*Mujer.*" He looked down at his paper.

"You think this is my fault."

"Ahh." He waved his hand dismissively in the air and got up from his stool. "You're not going to listen to anything."

"*¡Venga acá!*" she demanded.

"I'm going to read in peace."

Her elbow cracked when she lobbed the paper ball at his head. It bounced off his ear and landed somewhere on the other side of the breakfast counter.

They stared at each other for the longest two seconds that clicked by on the kitchen clock. Then he looked away, his eyebrows knitting together as he saw something behind her.

"What?" she demanded.

The newspaper hit the counter, and he stalked into the kitchen to lean over the sink to stare out the window.

"What's wrong with you?"

He waved her over without turning.

"Why don't you . . . oh God."

Susan wouldn't have believed her own mother if she'd told her that Tamara maneuvered a huge moving truck through the streets. *By herself.*

But standing beside John, she watched it with her own eyes.

"John—"

"Shish!"

She swore she heard the blood rushing clear out of her head as the yellow giant turned carefully into the driveway. What if Tamara couldn't see over the wheel? What if the seat was too high for her foot to reach the brake? What if she gave it too much gas and came ripping through their garage?

"You have to go out there and stop her."

"No, no." She heard a quiet pride in his voice. "She's got it."

"But—"

He grabbed her hand. She hadn't realized she clutched the arm of his T-shirt. "She's doing fine. Look."

He was right. Tamara slowed it to a delicate stop, the headlights beaming straight at them.

Pride glimmered as the driver's side door opened, and Tamara jumped out of that yellow monster.

She did it, Susan thought. *She did it without her father, her brother, or Ruben to guide her.*

But for what?

How could she be proud of someone who deliberately walked away from everything her own parents gave her? Sneaking around behind their backs, lying to them, embarrassing them in front of everyone they knew.

John looked at her when she pulled her hand free. "Come with us, mi vida," he pleaded softly. "Don't do this."

The front door dragged open, and Susan ignored the knowing lift of his eyebrow.

"Hi." Tamara rubbed her hands together, looking up when she saw them standing at the sink. "I didn't hit anything."

"We watched you." John leaned on the counter. "How come you didn't say anything about that truck? I would've gone with you."

"That's okay. But I think I might've overestimated the size," she said grimly. "What do you think?"

John chuckled, indulgently, like he always did in Susan's opinion. "You went a little big."

"Do you think I should take it back?"

Money wasted already, Susan thought. Just like she predicted.

"No, just leave it," he said. "I'll cover the extra cost."

Her frustration erupted, and she slammed her fist on the counter. John pivoted with the warning look he knew irritated her to no end.

Susan stabbed a finger in Tamara's direction. "I want that thing out of my driveway by eleven-thirty when Josie comes to pick me up."

"But I won't have a lot of—"

"Eleven-thirty," she insisted.

Tamara's eyes glistened, making Susan's heart pound harder. "And not a second longer, do you understand?"

Wide-eyed, her daughter nodded. "You're not coming with us?"

"No," Susan snapped, turning to the sink. "I have a barbecue to go to."

"Where?"

"Your Tía Josie's house. Why? You obviously don't want to be here or anywhere near anyone who knows you."

The fluorescent light buzzed over their heads. Memo's footsteps slowed to a stop in the hallway.

"Yeah, well," Tamara said, wiping her hands on her shorts while keeping her eyes glued to the floor. "Umm. I'll just go and . . ."

"Yes, you go." Susan's heart broke all over again. "Go away so your family won't butt into your life anymore."

Tamara fled the kitchen.

"I wish you knew who you just sounded like now," John said, giving her one last disappointed look before he walked outside.

"This is it," Tamara said, snapping the last lid onto the last plastic container.

Isa stood in the center of what had been Tamara's bedroom for all of her twenty-six years of life. "I can't believe you're really leaving."

Tamara tried not to see the sadness that weighed Isa's shoulders down, tried not to feel that she was abandoning her best friend.

Her bed lay stripped bare. The late-morning sun penetrated the slats of the window shades, threatening to turn the room into a pink oven.

"It's not like L.A. is on the other side of the country," she said. "You're coming up to visit me, right?"

Isa nodded. "I'll try. But with Andrew it's . . ." She shook her head. "Are you sure you don't need any more help while I'm here?"

"No. Are you sure you don't want to come up with us? Bring Andrew."

"I have to go to the barbecue." Tamara saw Isa's fear of being there without her. "Yolanda called me last night about it, and she wants me to make sure Carlos and Andrew are there."

"Has Carlos been around?" Tamara asked cautiously.

"Not really. But we had dinner the other night. Just the two of us."

"So is he going with you and Andrew today?"

Isa shrugged, her arms falling limply at her sides. "I think so. His mother gave me the what-will-they-say lecture if he doesn't show."

"You're not his mother."

"I know, but you know what it's like."

Oh yes Tamara did. Very few could understand the delicate maneuvers around *que diran,* what will they say?

Que diran was all about protecting the family image from *they*—family and friends who knew everyone else's business anyway. Since they were going to talk, you wanted to put a spin on things. By choosing this day of all days to move—Tía Josie's carne asada barbecue—Tamara was not only heaping the fodder for the *que diran,* but also leaving Isa to the mercy of her in-laws.

"Yo! You ready?"

Tamara and Isa turned around to see Memo leaning forward through the doorway with his hands braced on both sides of the door.

"It's gonna be different with you gone." He frowned at the empty room.

"Thanks," she said. "I mean for everything. You've been really cool."

"No prob. You want me to carry that out?" He bounded over and picked up the plastic container. "I owe you for that time you let me sneak into the house through your window."

"Next time you stay out past curfew you're on your own."

"Whatever, dude." They shared identical grins. "At least this time I can crash at your pad when they're mad at me."

Memo lifted the box over his head as he passed through the door.

"Did you—"

Tamara already knew what Isa was about to ask her. She shut the bedroom door behind her. "I'm going to tell Mom good-bye. You'll keep an eye on her, right?"

Isa rolled her lips back. She always did that when she was trying not to cry. They hugged to make up for the time in between now and whenever they'd see each other again.

"I'll call when I get up there," Tamara promised.

"Drive safe and be good."

"Memories, in the corner of my mind," Memo sang as he hurried out the door.

"Memo, what have we said about that?" her dad demanded, from his chair in the living room.

"Sorry, Dad," Memo drawled. "Misty watercolored memories of the way we were." One last wavering note, and he let the door slam behind him.

Tamara and Isa rolled their eyes. "Why don't you take him up with you?" Isa asked. One last hug, and Tamara watched Isa follow Memo outside.

With a rustle of his newspaper, her dad stood. Tamara was going to miss that sound.

"You have your keys?" He tapped the folded paper against the edge of his shorts.

Throat now totally swollen, Tamara nodded as she showed him the keys in her hand.

"Good. You've got your cell phone?"

She patted her backpack.

"What about money? You'll need some to get food—"

"I've got enough. Don't worry," she managed.

"Come here," he said roughly, opening his arms to enfold her.

She felt his chest shake as he breathed in. His strong arms held her tight, and she didn't want to go. For a moment the world was the safe beat of her father's heart, the pressure of his arms against her back, and the smell of Zest soap.

He patted the back of her head, then let her go. "Go out and say good-bye to your mother," he said. "She might not say anything, but it'll be best if you tried."

Tamara looked past his broad shoulder so he could wipe his tears away. Finally trusting her voice, "Maybe when things are better, you and Mom can come up and see my apartment."

"I don't—" His voice caught, then he cleared his throat. "We'll see. Go on. I need to make sure Memo shut the truck right."

Tamara heaved open the sliding glass door and followed the path of Mexican pavers, some concaved and worn, that led through her mother's dense forest of potted fruit trees and plants. A flat of mint rested on a table that listed to the right. Although old enough to be felled by a strong wind, the table was believed to have belonged to her mother's great-grandmother. The woman was reputed to have been a *curandera* and so it remained with the hopes that the spirit of her curative powers somehow seeped into its rickety old legs.

Her mother didn't look up from her tomato plants, which sagged with swollen fruit. Tamara felt a jittery coldness deep in her chest even though the late-morning heat wrapped itself around her.

"Well I'm off," she said. "We should be in L.A. by one. Dad and Memo are driving the U-Haul back to the—"

"Have a good trip," her mother interrupted. Her clippers cut through a stem, and a tomato fell into the pile of cilantro, chili peppers, and avocados she was collecting in the skirt of her apron.

Biting down on her bottom lip, tears stung Tamara's eyes, and her throat was tight enough to make breathing hurt.

"What, Tamara?" Susan turned around. "Don't you have somewhere to go?"

"I wanted to say good-bye."

"Good-bye."

Tamara balled her fists to stop the pain throbbing in the palms of her hands. "I'm sorry for all this. I didn't mean for it to be this way but—"

"Don't. *No eres mi hija*," she said without so much as a flicker of feeling. "My daughter would never speak to me like you did, nor would she throw her family away and everything they'd ever given her like trash."

"I said I was sorry." Her voice climbed an octave. Sometimes she wondered if her mother enjoyed making her cry so she'd remember her inferiority.

"What you did was unforgivable."

"Is this the way you want it? To part like this where we don't talk?"

"No, Tamara," her mother said. "That's how *you* want it."

Susan turned her back to her, her old tennis shoes padding quietly off the crooked path onto the grass toward the cucumbers trellised against the fence.

Tamara walked back into the house, then out the front door. For the first time in her life, she left her mother's home not knowing when she'd be back.

11

"YOU CAN SEE his command of the brush."

"But it's almost too controlled as if he . . ." the woman next to Will paused, making some artsy-fartsy circling gesture with her hand.

Listening to those two, he suppressed an eye roll.

"As if he paints without passion. There's no heart in this work," the woman declared, as if the canvas were a thing. Like it wasn't the artist's gut-wrenching creation, the one he'd stayed up all night to perfect the angle of a hand or agonized over the placement of a shadow.

This was exactly why Will had come to say no to Nadine Frazier.

He didn't want these tight-assed art critics who were either jealous they couldn't get their brush to obey or just plain didn't know what they were talking about, tearing apart his work.

"You see, I told her this artist wasn't ready to show." The woman sighed. "He's all technique, and he'll be over with—in five years."

"I've heard he's big with the industry, you know that young man, the one who directed that car movie. He loves him."

"Exactly my point."

Will didn't belong here. He didn't belong in a place where these people walked from one canvas to the other, picking apart and second-guessing everything the artist did.

And whoever this guy was, he painted with heart. If those people looked closer at the Botticelli-inspired girl holding the dead bird in her cupped hands, they'd see questions brimming in her eyes. They'd see how her hand gripped her pink skirt and the way she stood there with one foot turned inward as she held death for the first time.

If they didn't like what this guy did, they'd crucify the paintings in Señora Allende's garage. They'd probably buy them and then burn them in the parking lot outside the gallery so the world would be better off without them.

"Oh excuse me," the woman said to him. The gallery lights reflected in her glasses. "Would you take this away?"

Will looked down at the empty wineglass she held out to him. "No."

The old man standing with her took her elbow protectively. "Say now—"

"Server's over there." He pointed to the red-cheeked girl balancing a loaded tray of champagne through the crowd.

They exhaled a collective breath. "I'm so sorry you looked like a waiter dressed like . . ."

He turned heel and walked to the other side of the

gallery. *Dressed like what? Like he had a bike stashed out by the back door and a wife and litter of kids waiting in some ghetto apartment?*

Dammit, he paid seventy dollars for the pants and threw in another fifty for the button-down shirt.

Will found Nadine standing with a woman who gestured to one of the canvases—one with little boys chasing each other with slingshots and mice heads. She glanced at him, then nearly jumped on the heads of her guests to get to him.

"Thanks for waiting," she said, pulling him deeper into the crowd. "So what do you think?"

"It's cool."

"Cool?"

He stuck his hands in his pockets. "I've been thinking about your offer, and I'm not sure."

"Not sure about what?"

"This is all"—how could he say this and still be a man?—"real nice."

Nadine didn't seem to like the word "nice."

"I just don't think this is for me," he said.

"I saw you standing by my mother just now. What did she tell you?"

Will mentally groaned. What was it with women and their psychohypersensitivity about every tiny thing?

"Never mind," Nadine snapped, pushing her glasses up. "Forget it. You don't want to show your paintings here? Fine."

"It's not that I don't like your gallery. I like it a lot." Will had no idea what hole he had just fallen into, but he sure as hell was going to get out. "I'm not ready to do something like this."

He caught her studying him. Her jaw worked; he imagined her teeth grinding into dust in her mouth. "You know what I hate more than my mother being here tonight?"

Will braced himself.

"I really hate people who have a gift other people would kill to get but have no determination to use it. Why are you even painting, Will? Why fill up my nana's friend's garage with all those canvases?"

He held on to his silence, his eyes boring straight into hers. Nadine didn't flinch.

"Thanks for your offer," he finally said, offering his hand. She just raised her eyebrows as if wondering what he was still doing in her gallery.

Would this night never end?

Tamara's shoes gave profound meaning to the word agony. And her mind would never forgive her for the mindlessly repetitive music that blobbed all night long. She'd have nightmares of it for the rest of her earthly life.

But at least nothing had gone wrong. The evening, so far, was a success. Armed with the red dot stickers in her pocket, Tamara hadn't missed marking a sold painting while making sure used glasses and plates vanished before Nadine—or worse, her mother, Cynthia—noticed.

So why was she missing home? Her studio at the Mariner's Arms Apartments off Figueroa Terrace had that Raymond Chandler feel. And if she stood up on her toilet, craned her neck approximately thirty degrees, she could admire the downtown skyline.

Except the other day she actually got a view of a homeless man pooping, yes pooping, in front of the Dumpsters.

And then to add insult to injury, some overzealous meter maid left her a ticket. *Damn cops,* she thought again. Didn't they have real crime to fight?

This is what you wanted. Buck up. Make some small talk . . . network.

Pulling her shoulders back, Tamara turned to do just that when she saw him walking straight at her.

The music, the heat of the people, her tortuous shoes sucked out of space and time. She momentarily forgot how to breathe, as her brain frantically reasoned that it had to be someone who just looked like him.

Before she had a chance to crawl under a table——or, at least pretend she hadn't seen him——he saw her.

"What are you doing here?" Will asked.

Tamara breathed in. The room and its sounds were sucked into a vacuum. Her heart did a *thum-thump* and kicked into a rapid-fire patter.

"I work here." She tucked a piece of hair behind her ear, wishing she had a martini in the other hand instead of the stupid roll of stickers. "Hi to you, too."

He glanced away as if he wanted this awkward moment to go away as badly as she did.

"So how are you?" she asked.

"Good. You?"

"Busy. I work here as a gallery assistant. I just moved up here last week." She sounded like one of those dolls you pulled the string from the back, and it just blathered on till it droned to silence.

"I also work next door at the coffee shop at night," she kept going. "Just until Nadine decides she wants to keep me full-time."

It should be a crime for a man to look that good, she thought. Her cheeks darkened as the memory of that stupid, idiotic mistake of a kiss struck her like a clapper hitting a bell. What she wouldn't give to take back that whole episode so this could be the first time they'd met since high school. So he'd look at her like he had that night she gave him a piece of cake, not like he did now.

"So I take it Ruben didn't buy you a ring," he said.

She felt about two inches tall under his stare. What would Wonder Woman say in a situation like this? Nothing came to mind.

Improvising, Tamara stabbed her fists against her hips and lifted her chin. "Obviously."

Will hoped his expression gave nothing away.

"So what are *you* doing here?" Tamara asked, tucking her hair behind her ear for the fifth time. The blond streaks were gone, and it was back to its natural black. She wore it the way he liked a woman's hair, softly curled, so he could tunnel his fingers into it as he kissed her senseless.

He swallowed, remembering she'd just asked him a question. "Nadine invited me."

"Really? I didn't see your name on the guest list."

He struck her with another one of his hard stares so she wouldn't see that she could get to him. But she met his eyes straight on. "We met through mutual friends."

"Oh. So you didn't come for the art."

"Kind of. It's pretty good."

"Ralsh reminds me of Botticelli with a little of Edward Gorey's humor," she said, glancing around as if he bored her. "Did you know he started as a plein air painter?"

Was she doing this to make him feel stupid? If Will remembered correctly—and since he thought about it at least five times a day he was pretty sure he did—he wasn't the one who was drunk that night and kissed her. As he could recall, it was the other way around. "Yeah, I read the catalog, too."

"That's nice to know," she said. "I wrote it."

He thought he did a good job of not showing how much that impressed him. "Congratulations."

"Thanks," she said, as if he and his compliment didn't matter.

Tamara jumped when some dude with yellow hair placed his hands on her waist. *"In Bed* #2 just sold," he said in her ear. "We're going out to this after-hours place. Come with us and bond with the beast."

Even though he had no right, Will nearly slugged him. But Tamara seemed okay with this guy all over her, nasty pick-up line and all. He wondered if she'd kiss him on some bench, too.

The guy noticed Will, his eyes doing a quick once-over. He stepped out from behind her, holding his hand out.

Hello," he said smoothly. "I'm Jesse."

Will considered crushing his hand into a bloody sodden mass. "Will Benavides."

Jesse's blue eyes nearly bulged out of his head. "So you're the one! My God, Nadine's been gushing about you for days." He frantically searched the room for her. "Have you talked to her? You must talk to her, she's dying to . . ."

God, this was like one of those nightmares where he looked down and realized he was holding his dick in his hands with his bare ass flapping in the wind.

"I talked to her already," Will said, ignoring Tamara. "I'm just heading out."

Jesse's babble ceased, and he looked at him with mouth formed into an O. "And? Are you?"

"No."

"Oh no. Why?"

"Why what?" Tamara asked.

Will went completely still.

"Keep up, chick," Jesse drawled. "Nadine invited him to show his paintings here."

Her face lit up. "You're a painter? Why didn't you say any—"

"You know him?" Jesse asked, planting a hand on a thrust hip.

"We went to high school together," she said shyly.

"Then talk him into saying yes."

If she lifted her skirt to let Will see if she was wearing those sexy thigh-high nylons, she'd have no problem getting him to say yes.

"Bring him with us tonight," Jesse insisted, placing a finger on his chin. "We'll beat him into saying yes." With that, Jesse patted her shoulder, gave him a narrow-eyed glare, and left.

Tamara closed her eyes and took in a deep breath. "I have absolutely no idea what to say," she said.

"Awkward isn't it?"

That got him a grin.

"So did you put this whole thing together?" he asked.

She nodded, then shrugged. "Not by myself. I just called the caterer and the valet guys . . . it's not a big—"

"You did a good job."

She sighed, turning those brown eyes on him without any bullshit.

"I know what you think about me, but I'll say it anyway." He could see the pulse kicking in her neck. "I never got a chance to apologize for . . . well, you know. I don't usually drink, and I was upset about a lot of things, so I hope you don't think I go around doing stuff like that all the time."

Will balled his fists in his pockets as all the things he cursed her for that night came back at him.

"It's cool," he said oh so eloquently. "I shouldn't have uh . . . you know, got mad like I did. And I know you don't do that kind of thing all the time, okay?"

"Okay." Her grin bloomed into the full-blown smile he could never make himself forget. "That wasn't too bad was it?"

"I guess not," he said, wondering what else he could say that would make her smile like that at him.

"I should go." She hesitated, then held out her hand. "If it's too weird, I'm sure they'll understand if you don't want to come to this club tonight."

He took a deep breath, not wanting to let go of her hand, which felt so delicate in his. "How long have you worked here?"

"Two weeks."

She'd hooked into him without even trying. "Actually I'd like to go," he heard himself saying.

She blinked as if she expected him to say no, caught herself, and smiled. "Good. You can tell me about your paintings."

Will knew he was done for.

12

"**H**ERE, LET ME show you how to beat her."

Feeling brave, Will slipped off the barstool and walked over to where Tamara had been playing Holly, Jesse's accountant girlfriend, in the worst game of darts he'd ever seen. Most of Holly's had stuck out of the wall, even one in the floor. Two of Tamara's had hit the outer rim of the board, the rest the wall.

She held the dart over her shoulder with a grin. "Are you telling me that I suck?"

"You suck!" Jesse shouted, barely keeping his ass on the stool.

Ignoring Jesse and the way Tamara's teeth raked over her bottom lip, Will took her wrist and moved her fingers over the dart.

He felt her stiffen. She'd done that earlier when they walked into the bar and her shoulder brushed his chest as he held the door open for her. She'd been friendly and seemed to like talking to him, but for whatever reason, she didn't like him touching her.

"Okay, you hold it like this." He let go of her wrist, and he saw her shoulders relax. "Now step to your right so you're not aiming the dart straight at the board."

"Got it."

"Okay, now try it." Knowing for sure she didn't want him around, he took a long step back.

She threw her whole shoulder into it, and the dart bounced off the metal frame, rolling on the floor.

A roar of awwws swept through the crowd. Tamara laughed, holding her hand to her forehead. "At least I hit the board!"

"It takes practice," Will said, when she looked at him.

"You suck!" Jesse yelled from the bar. His friend caught him before he landed on the floor.

"Thanks, babe," Holly called, pushing her straw-colored dreads out of her face.

Will tried to figure them out. He could've sworn the dude was gay, but then with her black fatigues stuffed into lace-up Doc Martens and matching spike-studded leather cuffs, Holly did have the whole man thing going for her.

Tamara bumped into him softly. She'd only had one beer and hardly drunk three sips from it. He'd watched in case she needed him to drive her home.

"That's it. I'm too drunk!" Holly screamed, holding her hair in both hands after her dart thunked into the wall.

"Does that mean I won?" Tamara asked, looking at him wide-eyed with shock and delight.

"Not really," he said.

"I still luv you baby," Jesse crowed, as Holly wrapped her arms around him. This was definitely a different crowd than he was used to. Not that Will had a crowd he belonged to in the first place. But still, with the impressive tats and hardware pierced into their faces, it was real different.

"Isn't this place a trip?" Tamara asked, sliding onto the stool he'd been sitting in.

Will took in the authentic, old-school L.A. vibe. Built for serious drinking, the antique bar dominated the long, narrow room, and came with a chinless bartender, laughing at something Jesse said. The place didn't even have a name or a sign above the door. Plank floors creaked underfoot, four bloodred leather booths stood under the sidewalk-level windows, and art deco lamps cast a dim, reddish glow over the crowd. *Classic Edward Hopper,* he thought.

"Amazing how a place like this could still be around," he commented, taking the other stool because she seemed to want him to sit with her. Only when he did, no one seemed to know what to say.

"So how long have you been painting?"

"About five years. I didn't paint much when I was in the Marines."

"What did you do in the Marines?"

"Fire duty. Got my AA degree."

"Did you like being in the Marines?"

He reached for his beer glass and sipped. "Yeah, it was okay."

This was starting to feel like an interrogation. He probably still believed she was a mindless drunk who jumped on strange male laps every chance she got. Or worse—maybe he thought she was boring.

The only thing Tamara knew was that every time he touched her, her hormones spiked, and something had to be done about it. She was a free girl. If she wanted to go home with him, she could, and no one would call her mother in the morning to report it.

Not that she would take him home. She wasn't that kind of girl. Yet.

She made a lap with her finger around the ring of water left by his glass, summoning her courage. "Can I ask you a question?"

She arched up to check his reaction. Not much to work with there.

"Sure."

God, the man had beautiful fingers. She shifted her hips when she remembered how they felt sneaking under her skirt.

"How did you end up on that 'just say no' mural project? I thought you might have beat someone up, but then I—" Ugh. Her nerves were all jangled up by this itchiness for him, and as a result, she was babbling. A Chatty Cathy would tell her to shut up. "So what did you do?"

He grinned, and she let out the breath she'd been holding. "I got caught giving Johnnie Muñoz a tattoo."

"Really? Where? On his butt?"

His eyebrows shot up, and those gold eyes of his widened like he couldn't believe what she said. Well, that made two of them.

"Sorry." She wished she could just slink off the stool and into the crevices of the wood floor. "Saying stupid things is a compulsion of mine."

He laughed. A bit shyly, but it counted. Her shoulders relaxed, and she lost the hamster-in-a-wheel feel in her stomach.

"Wow," she exclaimed. "You really can laugh."

"Excuse me?"

"You're kind of scary—I mean serious. But not in a bad way."

"Thanks. I think," he said, still smiling. "Now I get to ask you a question."

She immediately thought of him and her on that bench when they kissed. "Oh." She forced a grin, then took a drink. "Okay."

"What're you doing up here?"

Damn, he didn't want her to take him home. Then again, thank God he didn't want to. "I guess I took your advice."

His left eyebrow cocked. She'd noticed he did that instead of ask a question. "Remember how you told me it took you four tries to get into the fire department? So I figured I'd try again to get into USC, but—"

How corny could she possibly sound?

"But what?"

"I don't know." Feeling on the spot, she tried to make herself smaller by stuffing her fists into her lap. "I guess I wanted to see what I was made of."

"Sounds like a good reason to me."

Looking at him smile, Tamara knew she had to figure out how to see him again. Maybe she wasn't *Sex and the City* material, but she wasn't a total dud.

Will glanced at his watch. "I have to be in early tomorrow."

"I should go too."

She said her good nights to Jesse, who had both legs around Holly. He made a growling sound when he saw Will behind her, and Tamara immediately liked Holly when she elbowed him.

Vaguely she remembered saying good night to every-one else. During that long trip to the door, she kept think-ing how to proposition Will.

And now that they were on the sidewalk, walking past the caged-in electronics stores and the bums huddled under cardboard and plastic trash bags, she had her chance. Maybe not her ideal setting, but a girl had to make do.

"Hey, I was thinking," she said, balling her hands in her coat pockets. "Since I'm new to L.A. and you've been here for so long that maybe we could get together, or I might— I mean, you, might rope me—*show me* the ropes."

He stopped, and she knew this was it. He was going to read through the lines and kiss her again. In this moment, Tamara Contreras forever did away with that wimpy mama's girl who believed men should be making the moves. She was a role model for Latinas everywhere—

"I can't," he said gruffly.

"Oh."

And in this moment, Tamara knew she had way too lit-tle alcohol to handle this level of humiliation.

"I'm seeing someone."

Pop went her ego.

"Heh." She took a big step backward. "That's great. I hope she's a good person."

His eyes looked off to the side. The traffic light changed behind her, turning his face red. "Yeah, she is."

Tamara stiffened her shoulders against the disappoint-ment. She stuck her hand out. "Okay, well, good-bye, Will. Good luck."

His hand sent heat straight to the center of her, and he squeezed just enough to make her knees turn to water.

The light turned green, and she thought she caught him looking at her like . . . Oh forget it. This wasn't like a Nora Roberts novel, where the guy secretly pined for the heroine. He looked at her like nothing.

"Let me walk you to your car," he said huskily, but did so leaving her phone number and virtue sadly intact.

TAMARA HAD STOPPED CALLING.

The weekly messages she left on the answering machine had at least reassured Susan that she was alive.

Then they stopped. Tamara called regularly at six o'clock on Wednesdays. John talked to her, and so did Memo. She heard them. But neither one of them said anything except when she overheard Memo telling one of his friends about some person named Jesse, who was Tamara's second boss.

Díos, when she heard that Tamara had a second job at some coffeehouse, Susan considered drawing up her will and giving everything to Memo.

How could Tamara have done that? Lied about this other job knowing that Susan and John worked their fingers to the bone so she could have a college education and a real career.

How could she serve tables when their ancestors fled the banditos of the revolution across the desert, the alligators of the Rio Bravo into Las Cruces, New Mexico, and broke their backs for slave wages so their children's children's grandchildren could have a better life?

And to do so when she should've been married and saving money so she could start having children?

Susan hustled down the windy hallway of the five hundred building. Outrage boiled her blood once again.

She had to get to the bottom of this, and the only person who could give it to her straight was sitting in her classroom grading papers.

Susan flipped her hair back, ran her fingers over her eyebrows, and mashed her lips together to make sure the lipstick was evenly distributed. She was armed for battle.

"Hello, Isa," she said, breezing into the sun-filled classroom. Inwardly she sighed at Isa's frizzy hair, the baggy T-shirt over the jeans, and the combat boots. How many times had she told her to throw those things out?

Ay, but what could she expect? With a mother like Dara, who ran out on her own family, Isa had no one to tell her how to dress or, God help them all, not to wear a black bra under a white blouse. Until, of course, Susan stepped in. But as quietly dignified as Isa could be, she had no fashion sense and no sense to do anything about it.

Isa jerked up from the papers she graded and silently rose from her seat. Her pen hit the desk, then rolled onto the floor.

"Hi," Isa said, finding her voice.

"How have you been?" Susan asked, taking her into a tight hug and planting a kiss on her cheek. "Sit, sit. How are you, m'ija?"

Isa sat down, giving her that look she'd seen a million

times when the girls had done something they didn't want her to know. "Fine. And you?"

"Fine, fine. We haven't seen you and Andrew lately."

Susan watched for Isa's reaction. *Nada.* This was worse than she thought. "Is everything okay?" she prompted.

"I'm just busy finishing up summer school."

"And where is mí Andrew?"

"He's with Yolanda."

"Oh." Susan could only imagine the daily hell Yolanda, bless her heart, put Isa through. "Well, that's good. And Carlos?"

Isa shrugged, and her gaze fell to her desk.

Tamara could wait.

"What's wrong, m'ija?"

A big sigh flushed out of Susan when Isa just shook her head. *These girls.* "M'ija, it will do you no good keeping all this inside." Susan waited for some reaction. "It's Carlos, yes?"

Isa nodded. "Yes and no. Yolanda came to the house the other day and—I shouldn't. You're friends, and I don't want to say anything."

Susan closed her eyes and breathed past the sadness she felt for this girl. That woman, Dara, left Isa and her father when Isa was just twelve years old, when she started that phase of life when a girl needed her mother the most.

Like now, when Isa's marriage was crumbling to pieces.

How Dara could leave her own daughter for some married car salesman in Phoenix Susan would never fathom. She thanked Papa Díos and Madre Maria that, unlike Dara, they'd given Isa the maternal instinct with Andrew.

"No, no. I know how Yolanda can be. What did she say?"

"She said if I left Carlos, she'd take away the house."

Susan sat straighter. "Why would she say something like that?"

"I don't know. I've tried with Carlos, you know I have, but she thinks"— Isa stared across the classroom—"I think she thinks I'm like my mother."

"Now that's not true."

"I got pregnant at nineteen like my mother did. I made a man marry me like my mother did," Isa said bitterly. "So that makes me just like her, doesn't it?"

Oh God, Susan thought. She'd heard those same words from Yolanda over and over again, never imagining Isa would overhear them.

"No matter how many times I try to tell her, I didn't get pregnant on purpose. I loved Carlos, but I wasn't trying to trap him."

"Isa, you don't have to tell me—"

"I was just stupid. I let him talk me into . . ." She shook her head. "I wish I didn't have to feel like I need to keep explaining myself."

Susan took Isa's ink-stained hand and squeezed. "M'ija, you don't have to explain to me."

A small smile touched her lips, then fled.

Susan's mother would die another death if she could hear her now. "M'ija, you can always leave him. I know how important it is to you to give Andrew a family and a home but Carlos . . ." She took in a deep breath. Butting into someone's marriage even if Isa was her girl, well it was delicate.

"Carlos will never change. And if Yolanda turns her back on you and Andrew, you have a home with us."

Isa's beautiful blue eyes filled with tears, and Susan steeled herself to stay strong for the girl. "You know, Tamara said the same thing," she said.

Hearing her daughter's name spoken was like a dash of cold water to the face. John and Memo never spoke it in front of her.

"What?"

"I talked to her last night. She said you'd say exactly what you said to me."

Susan had no idea what to say.

"She's fine," Isa said. "She likes her job and her apartment. I'm going up there to visit soon."

Susan released her hand and sat back. "Well. I'm glad. Do you want me to watch Andrew?"

"I thought about asking Carlos to stay home, but he'll probably drop him off with Yolanda."

"Bring him to the house. Memo has a soccer game, and we'll take him with us."

Isa opened her mouth and Susan drew herself together, knowing she was going to ask her to come up to L.A. to visit with her.

But she didn't.

"Thank you, Susan."

Well at least someone appreciated her.

"*De nada, m'ija. De nada.*"

14

AFTER HIS FOURTH and sure-to-be-final date with Kirsten, Will realized what he wanted. It must have been around the time when her friend's boyfriend called him Bill for the fifteenth time that night, or when Kirsten answered her cell phone for the eightieth time.

Didn't matter. After that one night with Tamara—one long month ago—Will knew he couldn't see Kirsten any longer. Even if it eased Señora Allende's mind, he just couldn't.

Instead he was going to go . . . well he hadn't quite figured that out yet.

Will set down the mallet, the broken avocado green tile fanned out on Señora Allende's bathroom floor, and peeled the goggles off his face. It didn't escape him that he'd worked himself into a corner, literally and figuratively.

All that mattered was that Kirsten would be sober and recovered from her hangover by tonight. He'd steeled himself against the delight in her eyes when he asked if they could get together again. He hated to get her hopes up because he was determined to end it face-to-face, like a gentleman.

"What have you done to my floor?"

Will's pulse spiked when Señora Allende's voice echoed above him.

She scowled down at the mess, purse dangling from one arm and a black mantilla draped over her shoulders.

"I thought you were at church," he said before she spontaneously combusted.

"And so you sneak in here and destroy my home?"

Even though the mallet rested against his thigh, he feared for his life. "It was old and needed to be replaced."

"Oh really? And who told you?"

He shrugged, rubbing his hands on his thighs. "I just thought I'd redo it for you. I'll have it finished by tomorrow afternoon."

She crossed her arms over her chest. "So you're replacing a floor that didn't need replacing when you have a painting that you haven't worked on in weeks, no?"

He knew better than to be surprised that she'd been keeping count. "I'm just trying to help."

"*Por favor, m'ijo.* Tell me why you're not painting."

"I just said—"

"No. That's not the real reason." She drew her shoulders back. "It makes you think about them, no?"

Sometimes he wished she didn't know him so well. "Yes."

"Then start another one." She paused for dramatic effect. "It's not like you have that gallery show to worry about."

Will held up his hands, then dropped them. He gave up. The woman knew everything.

"Did you know that you devastated that girl?" Señora Allende asked, pulling up the edges of her mantilla and getting a good steam going. "Broke her heart? Ruined her business!"

Ruined her business? He'd seen the work on those walls, and he hardly ruined Nadine by saying no.

"I wanted to tell you," Will explained, trying to stand up, but the blood rushing back to his legs shot needles of pain. He gave her just enough time to get good and worked up to start yelling at him in a babble of Spanish.

Getting yelled at in Spanish was worse than getting it in English.

She demanded to know why he said no, how could he say no, what business did he have saying no? Especially all that she'd done for him, making her comadre bring her poor nieta away from her work? Didn't he realize what people would think? What they'd say? They'd talk about it for weeks at the church; she'd be a laughingstock until Doña Alvarez's cross-dressing son visited again.

She switched to English. "There's a saying for people like you—"

"You don't know what it's like," he snapped, when she took time to breathe. "To have other people judge you, to just dismiss everything you've worked for. I didn't ask you to bring Nadine into my studio or to throw Kirsten at me, but I went along with it. Now stop trying to fix my life, because I liked it just the way it was."

She straightened up from the door, shocked he'd raised his voice at her.

"I see." The sharp lines of fury softened, making him feel worse. "If that's what will make you happy, then that's all there's to it."

They stood each other off, waiting for the other to make the first move. And then Señora Allende lobbed a grenade.

"Ricky would've been proud," she said, her voice deep with disappointment. "Ricky would've wanted this for you."

Yep. She always went straight for the jugular.

Well, if she was going to push him around, he wasn't going to take it sitting on his ass. He gripped the edge of the sink to haul himself up to his leaden feet.

He opened his mouth to say something about how Ricky was dead. He'd been dead for sixteen years and wherever the hell he was he wasn't worrying about some crap paintings in some vieja's dusty garage.

But then Will saw it and cursed himself for not seeing it until now. Her eyes were rimmed with old tears and her mouth bracketed with deep lines of sorrow.

"What happened?" he demanded, hoping one of her comadres hadn't died or her daughters hadn't called.

She made a dismissive hiss. "Don't change the subject."

He wondered if the problem was the man he saw leave the house. "Did someone upset you?"

She backed into the hallway, pulling up the edges of her mantilla. *"Te tengo que dar nada."*

I have nothing to say to you.

Now he really felt like crap.

"No, I do have one thing to say to you," she said. *"El bien no es conocide hasta que es perdido."*

With that she grandly exited the doorway.

He hobbled after her to the sala. "I'm sorry. I shouldn't have yelled at you."

She turned, her mantilla looking like black wings as she reached for the pocket doors.

Will glimpsed her Virgin statue standing quietly in a corner, her slender hands pressed palm to palm in prayer. With begrudging respect, Señora Allende placed Jesus slightly behind one of the potted ferns. She once told Will that sons had no place listening to women's business.

Señora Allende was the last person he wanted mad at him. Ever. He could take it when she chastised him, or when she tried to control him. But not speaking to him scared the hell out of him.

"I'm afraid," he admitted over the roar of the doors drawing to a close. "I said no because I didn't want—"

He took a deep breath not knowing how to put all the things that gnawed at him into words. Anger and loneliness he knew how to deal with, but all the other stuff, even happiness just . . . it made him tense up inside to the point where he couldn't even think straight.

"I went to that gallery and saw these incredible paintings that people just ripped apart." He paused, biting down on the pain that hollered through him as he imagined his work on those walls and those people gesturing at them like they had that night.

"M'ijo. Then why do you paint? If you don't want people to enjoy them, why?"

Will thought about Ricky, how he'd carefully paste Will's drawings on the walls in the countless apartments they'd lived in. How Ricky had signed him up for that contest at the library and the unbelievable joy they both experienced when Will accepted that blue ribbon for first place.

"I do want people to see my work—" He drew his hand over his mouth, wishing the one person he wanted most to see it was still here. "I just can't."

"*M'ijo, venga acá.*"

He did, keeping his eyes on the floor. When he got there, he took her in his arms and held on to her. Her tears were hot against his shoulder, and her trembling made him so aware of her fragility.

"Are you telling me you want to marry me?" she asked.

They both laughed, and he snuck a hand free to wipe away tears.

"Sorry, but your daughters will think I'm marrying you for your money," he joked.

"*Travieso.*"

He swallowed to loosen up his throat, then asked, "Are you going to tell me what you said? You speak really quickly when you're mad."

She patted his back. "Good things are not appreciated until they are lost, m'ijo." He felt her gather herself together, and he loosened his hold. "Do you understand why I tell you that?"

He nodded and cleared his throat. "Yeah I know."

"Don't yeah-I-know me," she scolded. "And I accept your decisions. But don't live your life wondering what people will say. You can't control what they'll do or say, but you can control how it gets here." She stabbed his chest. "*¿Entiendes?*"

A car whooshed by, and the songlike laughter of children playing next door drifted through an open window.

"I want to see you happy, m'ijo," she murmured. "You always look so lonely."

He took a deep breath and thought about Tamara.

"I have to meet Kirsten tonight," he said, figuring he might as well let her know the whole of it. "We don't, uh, click, and I'm going to tell her tonight."

When Señora Allende didn't react, Will held himself back to see what the holdup was. "What?"

"M'ijo, I don't think . . . why don't you call her and tell her over the phone?" This was about as close as she was ever going to get to admit that she had been wrong. And Will knew he should savor the moment, except he couldn't quite believe she was encouraging him to break up with her.

"I thought you wanted her and me—"

"Let me say it like this. Doña Alvarez's nieta was not brought up the way she should have been."

"I'd rather do this in person."

"Why?" Señora Allende asked cautiously.

"Because it's the right thing to do."

Señora Allende had been holding onto her breath. "You'll tell her nicely, yes?"

"I will."

"Where?"

"I told her I'd meet her for a drink."

She looked off to the side, thinking about it. And then she nodded as if satisfied with his decision.

"You should get back to work, m'ijo." Señora Allende dusted off his shirt. "I'll make you something to eat before you go."

"You don't need to—"

"Ah! You can't break up with a woman on an empty stomach."

Grinning, he didn't want to let her go. But he did for now.

Not long after Will took a shower and changed, he sat in the kitchen with Señora Allende while the news played from the sala. Times like this, they could be quiet. He could tell something was weighing on her mind, but right now he had his own problem: how to gently break things off with Kirsten without getting killed.

"M'ijo! Did you see that?"

He looked up from the meat loaf sandwich Señora Allende insisted was his favorite. "See what?" he asked. The backyard was filling with shadows as the sky turned what he thought of as saxophone blue. It felt good to be clean, but his nerves were a mess.

"Someone is in the backyard!"

He shot up out of his chair and crossed to the window over the sink. "Did you see who it was?"

"No. I saw him out of the corner of my eye." She stood right there beside him. "Did you lock your door?"

He never locked his apartment door when he was home.

"Stay inside and lock the door," he said, walking to the back door. She opened a drawer behind him, and he turned as she grabbed her biggest knife. "What do you think you're doing?"

"Come on. Let's go," she said, waving him to go on.

"No. I want you to stay in the house."

"Do you think I'll sit here if some murderer tries to kill you?"

"Call nine-one-one."

She reached around him and opened the door, marching outside.

It wasn't hard to catch up to her. "Stay behind me," he ordered.

"Walk faster then," she hissed.

Will peeked in the windows of his studio. It was empty save for the darkness.

His nerves jumped when she tapped him on the shoulder. "I think they're upstairs."

He strained his ears and heard what sounded like someone thumping against the floor. Every male protective instinct shot alive. "Go back in the house and call nine-one-one."

Señora Allende tightened her grip on her knife and reached into her apron pocket. She held up a cordless phone. "I'll call from up there."

Will knew if he tried bullying her, she'd only shove him out of the way and go *mano a mano* with what could be some druggie who wouldn't have any hesitation knocking over a seventy-six-year-old woman. And who wouldn't have a chance if he tried.

"I mean it, stay behind me," he insisted.

"¡*Vamanos!* Before they get away."

Will crept up the stairs, pausing when he heard a strange hollow spraying noise. He looked down at her over his shoulder, and she shook her head, no idea what that sound could be.

He jogged up to the top, yanked open the door, and swore he'd never think of whipped cream the same way again.

"Surprise," Kirsten sang, standing there with melted white goo running down her bare breasts and onto the tiniest red panties he'd ever seen in his life. "It's not really working, but look."

She aimed an industrial-sized can of whipped cream at her left breast. The can sputtered a few drops.

"What the hell are you doing here?" Will asked her, his voice unsteady with pure fury pumping through him.

"What do you think I was—"

Señora Allende shoved her way inside, and their screams filled the room. Kirsten frantically tried to cover herself with her hands. The can hit the floor and rolled to tap against his shoe.

"Get her out of here!" Kirsten shouted, half-bent over in a crouch.

"You see!" Señora Allende pointed the knife at Kirsten. "I told you she wasn't raised right!"

"Excuse me?" Kirsten straightened, planting her fists on her hips. "This is a private moment."

"*¡Escandalosa! ¡Es un disgracia en tu familia!*"

"Look old lady!" Kirsten stomped toward Señora Allende. "This is what young people do, and—"

"Enough," Will shouted, startling them both silent. "The bathroom is through there. Get your clothes on."

Kirsten looked at him like her heart was breaking. "But I—"

If she were anyone else, Will might be amused to find a naked girl with whipped cream all over her. But all he felt was disgust that she'd broken into his place.

"This was the wrong thing to try with me," he said. "Go."

"Not until she pays to clean the carpet," Señora Allende chimed in.

He turned to her, and, sheepishly, she lowered her knife. "Go downstairs. I'll deal with this," he said.

She raised her chin. "And leave you with that? Never."

"Fuck this shit," Kirsten screeched, pulling on her clothes. "I don't need no little boy who has to be told what to do by his grandma."

"Get out," he told her.

She made that stupid head move that drove him nuts. "Make me."

Will took a step toward her, and she stumbled back. She didn't see it coming when he ducked down, grabbed the backs of her thighs, and tossed her over his shoulder.

"What are you doing?" she screamed, as he walked out the door and down the steps.

Astonished, Señora Allende let him pass, then glued herself to his heels.

"I'll fucking kill you for this!" Kirsten shouted.

"Matilda, *que está mal—¡Ay Díos!*" Doña Villaseñor stood in the backyard wielding a frying pan that was nearly half her size.

She stepped aside for Will to walk past.

"What is he doing?" she asked.

"Defending the honor of his abuelita," Señora Allende declared. "Quick, call Barbara and Concha!"

The neighbors heard the screaming and they appeared in their doorways when Will pushed the gate open. Women screamed when he dumped Kirsten on her feet. Whistles and wolf calls pierced the night.

"Now go," he said, fists taut against his sides, no longer from anger but from the need not to laugh.

"You fucking bast—" Kirsten choked.

"I know, get in your car."

"Go fuck yourself!" She stood up straight, walking backward to her car. "This is the best piece of ass you'll never get!" And with that she slammed her car door and pulled off.

Behind Will Doña Villaseñor sighed. "Ay yi yi, what are we going to tell her abuela?"

"You see, m'ijo," Señora Allende said, patting his arm. "Now you don't have to break up with her. Everything works out for the best."

He turned to her, his arms and chest sticky from the melted whipped cream. "Next time you want to set me up with a girl, don't."

15

TAMARA COULD'VE SWORN she asked the woman behind the counter holding her bag of bananas if they had Roma tomatoes. The woman blinked her little brown eyes and burst out laughing.

Isa took in a deep breath, then stepped forward, expertly speaking rapid-fire Spanish to the woman who looked like she stepped out of a Diego Rivera painting.

They laughed. Tamara blushed. "You have no idea how much I saved your ass," Isa said, handing her a bag of tomatoes.

"Don't even tell me what I asked her," she said, when they drifted away from the stand and back into the chaos of Grand Central Market.

"It was pretty interesting," Isa said.

Tamara looked over her shoulder at the woman, who was still laughing and was now pointing at them with an old man. Los Angeles was a big city. She'd never see them again.

"If I don't practice, how will I learn?"

"Keep trying," Isa assured her. "Just not in public or alone. Did you get everything on your list?"

After they stored everything in the trunk of her car, she wanted to show Isa everything that made her fall in love with L.A.

They worked their way out of the parking garage and back into the chattering crush of the market. Piñatas hung from the ceiling, and the botanica stalls offered roots, powders, and some truly questionable substances in giant glass jars. Straw covered the crowded paths wedged between meat counters, vegetable stands, dollar Chinese, and a small tortilla factory.

She nearly had a heart attack when out of the corner of her eye she thought she saw Will.

"What?" Isa cried, when she jerked to a stop.

The guy was just a teenage boy with a platter of juice samples and eyes that tried to see through Isa's shirt.

"Nothing. I thought I saw someone."

"Who?"

"No one." She started walking again, feeling stupid for getting all uptight at the thought of seeing him again.

"Do you come here all the time?"

She heard the sneaky tone in Isa's voice. "Cool, huh?" They walked out the elephant doors and stood waiting for the light. "See that white building? That's city hall."

No one called her the master of changing the subject for nothing. If it hadn't been for a homeless woman scrubbing the almost black sidewalk on her hands and knees, Isa wouldn't have stopped her probing.

"So where are we going now?" Isa inched closer.

"Angel's Flight, then we'll see the fountains at California Plaza, and I'll take you to the building they used as SD-6 from *Alias*." Tamara nudged her to the crosswalk. "Do you want to see the new cathedral or Disney Music Hall?" She wrapped her arm over Isa's shoulders. "It only took you a month, but I'm so glad you came. I really missed you."

"You look happy," Isa said.

Unfortunately they knew each other for so long that it would sound ridiculous if Tamara said the same thing about her.

But Tamara wasn't sure how or when to broach it. "I am. Poor as dirt, which is what we're eating at my place, but I really like this city. It feels like home."

Isa's mouth clamped down shut when the signal turned green, and they went with the tide across the street.

Tamara paid the two-dollar fare for them to pile into the railcar with a stepped platform and polished wood benches with black posts and handrails. The track stretched up Bunker Hill, separated into two tracks, then merged back into one.

The car jerked upward, and Isa's hands clutched the edges of the bench.

"Why didn't we just walk up the hill?" Isa asked, as they slowly ascended.

"No one walks in L.A."

The wind lifted her hair off her neck, relieving the heat of spending an hour in the thick of the market. Lower downtown stretched into a bright hazy mass sharply divided by the hulking buildings that stretched skyward.

They arrived at the top of the hill and walked across the granite plaza that bridged the Hotel Intercontinental and two glass towers. Children ran along the edge of the fountain working itself into a crashing wave of oncoming water that would suddenly drop off into an invisible trough, giving you second thoughts about being washed off the plaza and down the hill.

Tamara found two empty chairs, and they sat down, relieving their arms and legs. The fountain exploded into its grand finale, sending children into delighted screams as the white water rushed toward them. And then it calmed into a lapping, gentle pool.

"When do you reapply to USC?" Isa asked.

"Soon. If I make the December deadline, I'll be eligible for next fall," Tamara said, feeling like they kept running out of things to talk about. "So I'm thinking as a backup that maybe I'll apply to Cal State Long Beach and San Francisco State."

"San Francisco? I thought you liked it here."

"I do but—" She took in a deep breath. Most of the time she didn't think about the precariousness of her future. And when she did, the anxiety that she'd given up a sure thing for complete uncertainty seemed unhealthy.

"I could keep working in the gallery and work my way up."

"But didn't you move up here to get your degree? I thought that was the whole reason for all this?"

Tamara heard the accusation in Isa's voice that she'd caused all this grief and now she was thinking about giving up.

"I know. And I want my degree because I'll have the option of working in a museum or going into art consulting." Her skin prickled under the shade of the buildings and the persistent wind. "But there's always a chance I won't get into any of those schools."

Isa stayed quiet. She'd been real quiet ever since she buzzed Tamara from the intercom outside her apartment building. Unless they were going to spend the rest of the day walking their carcasses around downtown in this awkward silence, she had to just get this out of the way.

"So what's up with you?" Tamara asked, having repeated the question whenever the conversation petered out between them.

"Like I said before, same old same old."

"You're quiet. What's on your mind?"

Isa crossed her arms over her chest.

"What? Did you finally leave him?" Tamara asked, assuming the shock would wake Isa up.

"Yeah."

Tamara nearly exploded into a million pieces. "When? How?"

"Tamara, I don't want to—" Isa paused, leaning forward in her chair and looking away before settling back down.

This was one of the rare moments, Tamara realized, when she was truly speechless. But it didn't last long. "All we've talked about is when I'm applying to grad school or where I'm taking you next, and you left Carlos? What happened?"

Isa hunkered down in her seat. Tamara bit back a sigh. "What do you think I'm going to say? Don't do it. Go back to him. Think of the family."

"Oh please! Leaving Ruben was easy for you. It wasn't easy for me."

Tamara picked up her chair and waddled over to sit directly in front of her. "That was a cheap shot, and you know it. Where's Andrew? What happened? Where are you going to live?"

Isa's lower lip pouted, and her eyes stayed glued to her lap. "He's at your mom's house."

"Are you staying there?"

Isa just breathed, making Tamara want to wrestle her out of the chair and pin her to the ground until she spit it out. And then finally the pendeja nodded yes.

"So what happened?"

"I drove up to the law firm where he used to work. The receptionist couldn't find him because she was new, then her boss came out to tell me that they had fired him back in May."

Tamara imagined plunging a knife deep into Carlos's chest and making him eat his own heart for not just hurting her best friend but his son, too.

"So I drove home so I could pack up my things and Andrew's things . . ." Her breath hitched, and Tamara saw her friend's heartbreak just by watching her face.

"Don't." Tamara snatched up her free hand and held on with all her might. "You don't have to say any more."

Isa's mouth trembled, but she squared her shoulders.

"He was there. With some girl. And I've been at your mom's ever since."

"When did all this happen?"

"Two weeks ago."

And no one told her! All this time Tamara had been worrying about small things while her friend was going through this.

Isa fought hard to keep her tears from falling.

"It's not like I've never seen you cry before," Tamara said, and Isa gave a laugh to cover up her grief.

"You inspired me to finally do this," Isa managed. "If you could do what you did while everyone thought you were crazy, then I can, too."

But Tamara didn't have a six-year-old boy to raise or major debts like car payments and credit cards to shoulder. And she wasn't so sure that it was a compliment Isa had just paid her.

"Maybe we should look for a place for you and Andrew this weekend," Tamara offered. "I have some money saved, and I'll loan whatever you need."

"No. I have enough," Isa said, wiping away her own tears. "There's a legal resource through the district that I can use to start divorce proceedings. I won't take any more of his mother's money, and I won't live in that house. I'll be fine. I am fine."

"I know my mom would love for you and Andrew to stay as long as you need to. She's been waiting for you to do this for a long time."

"You should call her," Isa said.

And her mother should've called her when her best friend and son moved into the house. But Tamara kept that thought to herself.

"You used to be better at changing the subject." They laughed, and Isa squeezed her hand. Tamara gathered herself together, refusing to be weak if Isa didn't want her to be.

God knows why, but the woman hated crying. She'd never once cried in school when they were kids, and as an adult Tamara had only seen her cry once, just once, when Isa found out she was pregnant. So in order to prevent an all-out sob fest, desperate measures had to be taken.

"You remember what I promised I'd do if you left Carlos?"

Isa turned a withering gaze on her.

"I promised myself I'd buy you a martini and a pair of crotchless panties. We're going to Hollywood."

"Crotchless panties? I don't think so."

"Thongs then. Definitely martinis."

"What about the cathedral?"

"You can't go get sexy panties after visiting God!" Tamara thought about it again. This was an emergency. God would understand. "But the Beauty Bar doesn't open till eight, so we have time."

Isa gave a rusty laugh that was something between a bark and a snort. Tamara hadn't heard her laugh, really laugh, in a long time. She wouldn't be surprised if Isa had forgotten how.

"How long have you been promising yourself you'd do this?" she asked, getting up when Tamara had already collected their bags.

"Too long, pendeja. Let's go."

Isa made a face like she sucked on an unripe lemon. But she tagged along anyway. "Swearing is a sign of a small vocabulary."

"You should take it up," Tamara said.

"With this divorce, I probably will."

16

THAT NEXT MONDAY MORNING a FedEx envelope slapped on the desk, fractions of an inch from giving Tamara a severe paper cut.

Tamara looked up to see Nadine standing over her. Behind her, gray fog drifted like ghosts through the downtown high-rises.

"Hi," she said, then gulped.

"Did you really call Menard and leave a message like you said you did?"

"Yes," Tamara said slowly. *What have I done wrong now?* "I called last week and yesterday."

"Did we receive her contract?"

"Not yet. I'll check today's mail."

"Did you even send it?"

"Yes." An artery, maybe a vein . . . whatever hopped in Tamara's neck. "I had it sent priority overnight like you asked."

"Did you call to make sure she got it?"

"Yeah, I—"

"She said she hasn't gotten it!"

Tamara felt like the bug that just looked up in time to see the giant shoe bearing down on it.

"Did. You. *Call*. Her?" Nadine ground out.

"Yes."

"Where's the packing slip?"

Tamara dived for the bottom file drawer. Pink slips exploded in midair when her FedEx file slipped and hit the floor.

"It's here," she squeaked. She pushed her chair back so she could gather all the slips. "I put it here where I always keep them—"

Nadine made a strangled sound in the back of her throat. Hoping she wouldn't turn to stone, Tamara stood up and held out the packing slip she'd addressed last week.

"Oh now you want me to do your job?" Nadine asked nastily.

"No. I'll call and figure out what happened."

Nadine gave her one last cutting glance and walked to her office.

Bitch. Tamara's throat ached with frustrated tears she refused to shed in front of that *floja, pendeja . . .* she couldn't think of anything else to call her. But she knew one thing: Wonder Woman wouldn't take this shit.

She left four messages with that pretentious moron who called her *little girl* the only time she actually answered her stupid phone.

Don't do it, Tamara warned herself. *Don't you dare let her see you cry.*

Blinking back tears she called up the FedEx site and

typed in the tracking number. Aha! That lazy, lying bitch Menard signed for it. She grinned maniacally as she clicked print, ready to thrust her victory in Nadine's face.

"May I talk to you for a minute?" Tamara found herself asking Nadine from the doorway.

"Did you track down the package?" Nadine asked, without looking away from her computer screen.

Tamara took that as a yes to her first question and sat down. "Yes. She signed for it on Friday at 8:37 A.M. Eastern Standard Time."

No laughs from the audience. "I left her another message," she finished lamely. "I just wanted you to know."

"Did you open the envelope I left on your desk?"

Crap.

Nadine tore her eyes from whatever she'd been reading. "I thought you'd want the application to San Francisco State's museum studies program."

Nadine, the woman who made Tamara wonder every day if she'd live to see another sunrise, had sent away for an application? For her? Why? And she really meant to say thank you except what came out was, "You actually like me?"

Nadine looked at her funny. "Why would you ask me something like that?"

"Well . . ." Gee, where should she start? "I don't seem to uhh . . . take care of things the way you want me to," Tamara said, rubbing her palms over her pants. "And even though I called Menard—"

"Meh-nard," Nadine corrected.

Tamara stiffened her spine a little straighter. "Even though I called her and left her messages, you thought I was lying—"

"I didn't say you were lying. I just wanted to make sure you did it before I chewed her ass for keeping me waiting this long before signing her goddamn contract."

"Oh. So do I now have a full-time job now that we're beyond the thirty days?"

Nadine looked down at her desk and exhaled a heavy sigh. "I don't want you to quit," she said. "Even though I lost my patience and told you the other day that you needed to go back to kindergarten, I think you do a good job."

Tamara almost made her repeat the words "good job" but listened quietly.

"Here's the thing. Knowing our next installment is only two months away, and I haven't been able to sign anyone, my mother is probably luring Menard back to her gallery to teach me a lesson."

Nadine cleared her throat. "I can't offer you a full-time job because I can't afford it. I might not even be open long enough to have another show."

"I'm sorry," Tamara breathed.

"Don't be." Nadine's hands plopped down on her armrests in defeat. "I try not to take things out on people like she does, and it fucking embarrasses me when I catch myself sounding like her."

"I know the feeling," Tamara ventured. This was starting to sound like one of those after-school specials when the nerdy girl and the popular girl realized they actually did have something in common. "My mom hasn't talked to me since I took this job."

"I wish mine would do that." Nadine considered it like a dream that would never come true.

Deflating into the chair, Tamara asked, "Why would she want you to close?"

"So I can come back and work for her. My mother doesn't like anyone in the family to have some enterprise that doesn't involve her."

That sounded eerily familiar. "What are you going to do?"

"Try to sign Menard before she does. If I can get that pain in the ass in this gallery after Ralsh, I'm a made woman."

"What about Will Benavides?"

Nadine made a rude sound. "I would've given my left boob to sign him, but he said no."

After a moment in which Nadine probably counted every hair on Tamara's head, she grinned, and said, "Let my mother have Menard. I know how we can get Benavides."

Nadine burst with industry, gathering papers off the desk and stacking them in neat piles. "I know some people to call who can talk him into signing with us. In about an hour you're going to drive over the contract to him. He won't be able to say no if we bombard him. It'll be perfect because there's that sculptor from Monterey who I heard isn't happy with the gallery she's at down in Laguna . . ."

Tamara was still stuck on the point that she had to go to Will's house. She could do this. It was her job to do this even though Nadine's babbling made no sense. It's just Will, she told herself. She'd kissed him; hell he even had his hand up her skirt, and so it wasn't like they were strangers.

"What do you think about San Francisco?" Nadine suddenly asked.

A second clicked by, and Tamara caught up. "I think it's a good idea. But my parents won't like it."

"It's an hour and a half plane trip, Tamara."

To her parents living in another area code was bad enough. Another county? Tamara didn't have the fortitude to contend with that scenario in this lifetime.

"I'm telling you, your choices are San Francisco or USC." Nadine tucked the phone between her ear and shoulder. "Think about it. And get me an au lait."

Tamara had half stood out of her seat when Nadine remembered. "Please."

AFTER SHE YANKED the parking brake, Tamara looked around the car wondering who was speaking in Spanish.

"Jesus," she muttered, realizing she hadn't heard one word of her Spanish language tape.

"*¿Podrías ayudarme por favor?*," the female voice asked. "*Busco un libro del Ernest Hemingway.*"

"*Ahh sí—*"

She stabbed the EJECT button and switched off the car.

"This is ridiculous," she lectured to her reflection in the streaked rearview mirror while running a finger around the rim of her lips. "I'm here to deliver a contract and leave. Okay?"

Okay. She nodded to herself.

The window squealed pathetically as she rolled it up. A lawn mower *burred* and cars *swooshed* down the street toward the secret on-ramp to the 110 Freeway.

Tamara glanced at the address she'd written on a purple sticky note, walking past one cute bungalow after another. The sharp tang of cut grass carried on the hot oven blast of air, typical of L.A. in the summer. If she hadn't seen the pooping man again in the alley, Tamara would've opened her windows at night.

Her heels scraped to a stop when she saw Will pushing a lawn mower across the small yard.

Her eyes blinked rapidly behind dark sunglasses, memorizing his wet skin and his T-shirt tucked in the back of his shorts.

Business, she told herself, *this is strictly business.* She was on a mission to help Nadine save her gallery from her meddling mother and get Will's paintings before an adoring public.

If Wonder Woman was here, she would . . . Tamara doubted even Wonder Woman could compose herself when faced with a sight as sexy as Will Benavides without his shirt on.

He looked over his shoulder and saw her. "Hi," Will said, his stare making her grateful for her sunglasses.

"Hi."

"I heard you were on your way." His eyes narrowed as he watched a low-rider car thump to a heavy bass beat.

She clasped her hands in front of her. She could do this without further loss of her dignity.

"I figured we might as well get this taken care of now." *Good, very good.* But then, "So I brought the original, which you'll have to sign but I won't be able to give you a copy right away because . . . You don't mind getting the copy in the mail, do you? Because I can drive it over in case you want it . . . right away and . . ."

"You can drop it in the mail," he said. "Or I'll stop by and pick it up from you."

"So you're going to sign the contract?" Tamara gripped her purse strap when he wiped his forehead with his T-shirt.

"I'll think about it." Will jerked his thumb over his shoulder. "The back gate's unlocked. Walk around the corner, and I'll meet you in the backyard."

He turned then walked up the porch steps, paused to pull the lawnmower's plug before disappearing into the mint green bungalow.

Walking in the direction he pointed to, she admired the little house, with its gleaming windows. Red, yellow, and orange roses burst under a bay window, while a park bench sat with potted geraniums and pansies on the tiny front porch. A set of hummingbird wind chimes waited for the wind. Not the kind of place she imagined a guy like Will living in.

As she pushed open the back gate, she hoped for the sake of her professional decorum that he'd at least put his shirt on. On the other hand, considering she had to go back to the demonic force known as Nadine, a shirtless Will could be Karma's way of balancing out life.

"You must be the young lady," a voice said in Spanish.

Tamara jumped, then caught her bag as it slid off her shoulder. She stared at two old women, both wearing flowered housedresses that buttoned down the front. One wielded a dishcloth like a weapon in powerful-looking hands; the other, an angelic smile, with her hands clasped demurely in front of her.

Tamara cleared her throat, all the Spanish she'd drummed into her head zapping to nothing.

"*Hola.* Uhh." Four-year-olds spoke better Spanish than she did. "*Como estoy* . . . I mean, *estás*—"

Giving up, she slowly explained, "I'm looking for Will Benavides."

"He's inside changing," the tough-looking one answered in English. "Who are you?"

Containing the urge to run, Tamara flashed a smile as she walked over with her hand held out. "I'm Tamara Contreras. I work with Nadine Frazier, and I brought his contract."

The old woman assessed her, then gripped her hand firmly. Still skeptical, she holstered the dishtowel into her apron pocket. "This is Doña Villaseñor, Nadine's abuelita."

Tamara took the delicate hand. *"Mucho gusto,"* she managed.

Still smiling, Doña Villaseñor said something that had the other one grinning broadly.

"Come inside. You'll have some iced tea."

Tamara obediently followed them across the patio.

The kitchen probably hadn't changed since the 1930s. A large stove and oven hunkered down next to built-in cabinets fronted with leaded glass. The pink-tiled counters were faded and chipped in places but clean, and the refrigerator with a rounded top hummed contentedly next to a doorway leading to a hallway with walls crowded with framed photos.

"I'm sorry, Señora, but I didn't get your name," Tamara asked the bossy one as she reached into the refrigerator.

"Matilda Allende," she answered, pointing to a tiny Formica table with two matching chairs. "Sit."

Doña Villaseñor was starting to freak her out with that smile on her face. But Tamara did what she was told and sat.

"Does Nadine always make you drive to a strange man's house?" Señora Allende asked as she poured iced tea.

"Matilda!" Doña Villaseñor exclaimed.

"No. I went to high school with Will." Tamara folded her hands in her lap. "Your home is very nice. Have you lived here a long time?"

Señora Allende plunked a glass in front of her, then sat in the opposite chair, regally resting one hand on top of the other. "Since 1942. You don't need to know how old I was when my husband bought it."

Tamara grinned, not knowing what to say next. So she sipped her tea and realized Doña Villaseñor stood behind her chair like Luca Brasi, waiting to strike at the right signal from Señora Allende.

"How long have you worked for the gallery?" Señora Allende asked.

"A little over a month."

"What do you do?"

"I'm the gallery assistant."

"Ahh. Will has been painting every day—"

"Oh, yes, ever since—"

Señora Allende sent Doña Villaseñor a sharp look, and they fell silent. This was really starting to creep Tamara out.

"So you're the assistant. What do you plan to do later?"

Tamara cleared her throat. "I'd like to get my master's in art history and museum studies." She searched for the resemblance between her and Will, but didn't see one. "Maybe own my own gallery."

"Do you live with your family?" Doña Villaseñor asked behind her.

Twisting in her chair, Tamara checked to make sure a gun wasn't aimed at her back. "No, they live in Sweetwater."

"They don't mind that you live up here by yourself?" Señora Allende asked.

Tamara twisted back around, searching for an answer somewhere between the truth and an outright lie. "A little."

"Do they know Will?" Doña Villaseñor asked.

Tamara wondered if she'd ever get a sip of her iced tea. "No, not really."

Señora Allende's left eyebrow arched as if the answer intrigued her. Before either of them had a chance to launch another question, Will appeared in the hallway.

All through his three-minute shower and changing, Will was tortured by thoughts of what Señora Allende and Doña Villaseñor were doing to Tamara.

And he suspected something was going on between them because while he was putting the finishing touches on the paint job in the bathroom, Señora Allende insisted he mow the lawn after a phone call from Doña Villaseñor.

He'd hoped for a chance to sneak Tamara past them, but somehow their ears heard them over the novenas. Just as he got one foot through the door, Señora Allende stood there with a finger pointed to the bathroom down the hall, silently ordering him away so she could get her hands on another female of marriageable age.

Now he found them sitting companionably at her small table, as if they didn't know two of his worlds—the real one and the fantasy one that included Tamara—had just come crashing into each other.

"Ahh there he is," Señora Allende exclaimed.

"Hello again," Tamara said, oblivious to the broad smiles of approval on both of the viejita's faces.

"We had a nice chat." Señora Allende reached across the table and affectionately patted Tamara's hand. "She seems like a very smart young lady."

"*Que muy bonita*," Doña Villaseñor said with a wink.

"Thank you for the iced tea." Tamara looked at him as if she didn't know what to do next. "But I should get back to work."

She had no idea they'd all but stamped their approval on her forehead and were about to throw her at him.

"Oh no," Doña Villaseñor exclaimed, resting her hands on Tamara's shoulders. "You don't have to leave so soon."

"Ah ah ah!" Señora Allende shot out of her chair. "You go with Will so he can show you his pictures, and *I'll* take care of this."

Will started, "But I ha—"

"No, no," Señora Allende interrupted. "Young people don't need old ladies like us around."

He caught Tamara looking at him for help. Doña Villaseñor patted her shoulders, and she stood up to walk to the sink with Señora Allende.

"Now run along," Señora Allende said, handing him a glass of iced tea. With her back turned to Tamara she gave him a stern look and lowered her voice to tell him in Spanish, "Leave the doors open."

"Thanks," he said neutrally. He started for the kitchen door, showing Tamara the way. She thanked them again for the iced tea, and he couldn't help but roll his eyes when the two comadres insisted she was more than welcome to visit them anytime.

As Tamara slipped past him, he caught Señora Allende and Doña Villaseñor looking as if picturing them on a wedding cake.

Suddenly Tamara stopped, and he nearly collided into her. "You don't have to show me your paintings if you"—she paused when he stood too close—"if you . . . I don't want to get in the way," she continued, lifting her chin to look him in the eye.

"You're not. I don't mind getting out of mowing the rest of the lawn," he said with a grin he hoped would make her feel at ease.

"Oh yeah. Right. Well, if it's all right with you then . . ."

He led the way to the garage, and he opened the side door for her.

"So this is your fortress of solitude, huh?" Tamara asked.

He couldn't help but grin. "Something like that."

She stood by the door, holding her glass with both hands. "Have you ever shown your paintings before?"

"Only a coupla times."

"Where?"

"Just at my school. Why don't you come over here? You can see better."

She came to stand with him before the sketched canvas of his mother, his brother, and himself. He still couldn't bring himself to touch it.

"I thought you'd want to see one in the making," he said, when she angled her head and stared. He scratched his arm. "What?"

She looked at him with such a smile. "You've come a long way from your 'Just Say No' period."

He laughed. "Don't take too much credit."

One of the things he noticed about Tamara was that she could smile with just her eyes. And seeing that, it felt okay to breathe and maybe to show off a little.

He walked over to his stack of canvases, wanting her to see the one he painted of Señora Allende last March. "I didn't take any classes until my last year at Cal State L.A."

"What classes did you take?"

"Drawing mainly." He swung the canvas around and held it to his chest. "Lots of life drawing but only a couple of painting classes."

"You didn't major in art?"

He shook his head, watching the way the light streaming through the window illuminated the gold in her hair.

She studied the painting of Señora Allende watching TV in her sala, then back at the one on the easel. "It's almost like a photo," she murmured, walking toward him. She reached out with her hand, then stopped. "Can I touch it?"

"I'm sorry?"

"The painting. If you don't want me to—"

"No, it's okay. Go ahead."

She looked at him shyly, then approached. He held his breath as her fingers traced the light of the TV illuminating Señora Allende's profile.

"How do you make them look so real?"

"With paint," he joked.

Her eyes snapped up playfully. "No shit."

The tightness in his stomach let up completely. She nodded, listening intently to his explanation about his lengthy sketching process that ultimately led to the finished piece.

"So what else do you have?" she asked.

"How long do you have?"

Her eyebrows came together, and her lips tightened. "Actually, I should get going."

"You have a lunch hour, right?"

"But it's only a quarter to eleven."

"Take an early one."

She looked fully at him. Doubt crept its slimy self up his spine as he wondered if he was her reason for thinking so hard about it.

"I'm hungry and you're hungry, so why don't we go together," he said, figuring he couldn't lose for trying.

He heard his heart pounding while the gears in her head churned.

"Okay. But I should call Nadine and—" He watched fascinated by the way she seemed to think out loud. "Where do you want to go?"

18

BY THE TIME they slid into the corner booth in the back room of Philippe's, Tamara no longer felt like she had to watch what came out of her mouth.

Will made her drive, claiming he'd always wanted to ride in a Karmann Ghia. He didn't make stinging comments when she made one wrong turn, then missed another as they made their way out of Solano Canyon, over the Harbor Freeway, through Chinatown toward the restaurant located down the street from Union Station.

Will made her see the city better than she had since she moved there. He put her at ease, even after all the embarrassing things she'd done in the last two times they'd met.

His jokes kinda snuck up out of nowhere, and he had this amazing ability to spot little things like the little Mexican boy tugging on his grandmother's purse for a slice of pie or the old Asian woman sneaking spirits into her coffee out of a dented flask. And when he wasn't studying the people around them, she felt his scrutiny on her.

"Is Señora Allende your grandmother?" she asked after swallowing the last bite of her French-dip sandwich. She balled her napkin, then tossed it with the remains of her lunch.

"No." He wiped his fingers on his precisely folded napkin. "We met when I rented the apartment over the garage."

"She acts like she is."

"Tell me about it. I only met my real grandmother when I was a little kid."

"Only then?"

"She's dead now." Will looked across the table with those unreadable eyes. "She didn't like my brother and me very much."

"My grandma didn't like my brother and me much either," she admitted. "She and my mom didn't get along. Especially at the end. I guess Grandma wanted my mom to stay unmarried and take care of her."

She reached for her soda.

"Didn't she want your mom to have a family?"

"No. My mom's brothers were married, so she wanted my mom to stick around and take care of her." Talking about this so openly made her realize how strange that was. "So when Mom didn't, she never let her forget it. Accused her of destroying the family and all that."

"How come it got worse before she died?"

Tamara shook her head, never having asked her mother the reason. "She didn't tell Mom that she was dying, and my uncles didn't tell us about the funeral, so . . ." Remembering it out loud made her realize how much that must've hurt her mother. Why hadn't she ever realized that before? "I think my mom's aunt finally told her where they buried her." Tamara shook her cup to loosen the ice.

"Families can be great, can't they?" he asked quietly.

She grinned, hoping he wouldn't notice that her eyes were wet. "They can be," she said. "I haven't talked to my mom since I left home."

He sat a little straighter. "Why?"

"She's mad because—" How could she possibly explain this? "Well it's partly my fault because she set me up to become a teacher at her school, but I didn't want the job, which obviously embarrassed her, and so when I decided to move to L.A. she took it like I was throwing all that in her face—" She cut herself off, thinking Will probably thought she was spoiled and selfish.

"I can see you as a teacher," he said, grinning.

"I sucked big-time. But thanks anyway."

He just tapped his fingers on the side of his cup.

Tamara couldn't remember the last time she talked to someone . . . really talked and shared. Isa had retreated to her quiet self even after Tamara dragged her to Frederick's of Hollywood, then the Hustler store when she refused the thong panties.

But at least she'd sent her home with a black baby tee with Hustler blazoned across her boobs and some penis-shaped mints called dick-tacs.

Weird that of all the people, Will would be the one she'd play counselor with. And it didn't feel all that awkward since she hadn't kissed or asked him out. That is until now as the silence yawned longer between them.

"I should get you back," she said after a long pause through which they both stared across the restaurant. "So are you going to sign the contract? I'll lose my head if I don't bring it back."

"Give me a few days," he said, standing up out of the booth.

She couldn't think of anything smart to say and had no idea what to do next. Shake his hand? Hug him? Kiss him?

"I'll call you," she finally said when they stopped at her car. "To make sure you don't forget."

Saying nothing, Will stared a hole straight through her head. The dry wind, heavy with the smell of bus exhaust, blew her hair into her eyes.

"Hold on a second," he said.

When she looked up, he stood close enough for her to smell the grassy scent of him.

He brushed the hair out of her eyes, holding it back with both hands. His eyes bore down hard into hers. "I didn't think I could do this the last time I saw you."

She felt those hands drop down and his arms went around her, drawing her close. They moved in unison, her head turning so that her cheek rested against his chest, and his nose dipped down into her hair. He accidentally pinned her arms to her side, but after a second's hesitation, she snaked them around his waist.

While downtown L.A. hustled, honked, and swerved around them, she was only aware of his heat, the ebb and flow of his breath.

"*Deseo besarle otra vez,*" he whispered in her ear.

She bit down on her bottom lip as his words flowed inside her, igniting her right where it almost hurt to keep her thighs pressed together.

"*Haré solamente qué tú deseas,*" he promised. Her Spanish

might be lacking but she only needed to know two words, *besar y desea*, to know what he meant. And the way he said them . . .

Her fingers curled into his shirt when his breath brushed against her skin followed by his lips, moist and so hot, pressed the sensitive flesh right next to her ear lobe.

She felt his legs spread farther apart, and as she looked up, he pulled her tighter against him so her stomach met with his hips.

He grinned down at her, little wrinkles toying with the corners of his eyes. His heat penetrated right through the starched cotton of her button-down shirt and the fabric of her slacks. Impatient with the tingling in her ear, the need to feel his bare hands on her skin, her breasts, in between her legs, she kissed him.

Their lips sought each other tenderly at first, reuniting a familiar taste and heat. Wet, pounding lust closed in from some hazy distance, driving her to demand more. In that moment, Tamara shared a kiss unlike any other, one that never wanted to be broken again, that promised more and whispered *I missed you.*

Damn she was in trouble.

"*Oy papí*," some woman catcalled behind him. Their eyes opened, and they were back on the street alongside Phillipe's just a block down from Chinatown. He smiled down at her as if to say, *I don't mind if you don't mind.*

So much for professional decorum, she realized, hiding her blushing face against his shoulder.

"I wish I didn't have to go back to work," she said.

She shivered as his lips stretched into a grin against her ear.

"When do I get to see you again?" he asked.

"Whenever you want." She made a face as she realized how desperate that sounded. "I mean, I'm not always busy so if you wanted to do something tomorrow or this weekend, chances are that I won't be busy."

Her embarrassment eased when he nuzzled against her head and spread his fingers over the base of her spine. "Good, because I wouldn't mind doing that again."

19

"**I THINK YOU** should suspend the canvases from the ceiling and spotlight from the floor," Tamara suggested.

Jesse flipped a dish towel over his shoulder, looking like a domesticated Spike from *Buffy the Vampire Slayer*, in a spotless white apron over a black muscle shirt and leather pants. "Sounds great. I have to go."

"Nonononono." Nadine lunged and grabbed hold of his arm. Two chairs stood in the windows flanking the main doors. Jesse had come over with soup for Tamara's dinner thirty minutes before she started her shift at the café when Nadine nabbed him in on her project.

"What about the sculptures?" Nadine asked.

"I like Tamara's idea."

"But they'll block the view inside the gallery."

"You realize I don't work here anymore, right?"

"But you're family, so you have to help."

"Cousin by marriage doesn't count."

All of the local artists were organizing an art fair in the

parking lot of their building the day after tomorrow, and Nadine had been pacing around the gallery chewing her fingers to the knuckle to attract people inside.

And she was just a bit unhappy that Tamara hadn't returned with a signed contract from Will. Almost a week had passed since they had lunch together. And he hadn't returned any of Tamara's calls.

Tamara took a deep breath and let it out slowly, feeling the sun warming her back. Clearly nothing was going to happen between them. And she was okay with that because if anything did happen it would be purely physical.

Determined to get him out of her system, Tamara stepped forward. "The canvases will draw a second look, and if we keep the doors open, it'll be inviting."

She won Jesse over. Not that it was hard. He wanted to get back to the café before Holly walked in to take the night shift. Nadine had what Tamara recognized as the I'm-thinking-how-my-idea-will-work-better look.

"Use two that have sold, so if anyone inquires, we can show them the pieces we have available," Tamara said, edging closer to where they stood. "More than likely we're going to have lookey lous anyway, and—"

"How do you know that?" Nadine asked. "It's not like you've been here long enough to know better."

Jesse sighed. "I'm going. Tamara, eat and give yourself five more minutes."

"Why won't you help me?" Nadine begged him.

He shook his head and pivoted. "Help is standing right next to you."

"But it's—"

The three of them stared at Will after he knocked on the glass door.

Tamara's heart plummeted to her stomach. Nadine shot to the door, twisting the top and bottom locks. Jesse looked at Tamara and grinned.

Will glanced at her, then focused on Nadine. "I wanted to drop this off." He handed her an envelope.

"What's this?" Nadine asked what Tamara was dying to know.

"Signed contract."

His eyes flicked up at Tamara. "Hi," he said, as if they hadn't kissed.

"See you in thirty," Jesse said cheerfully as he slipped out the door.

"Tamara, go," Nadine said, holding on to the envelope like it contained her future. "Will and I have to talk."

"But what about the display?"

"We'll move the sculptures tomorrow. Take your soup with you. It's making me nauseous."

It burned the way Nadine just dismissed her and hooked her arm through Will's. And burned even more that Will had said hello so casually.

Arms crossed tight over her chest, Tamara watched him stroll away with Nadine chatting about framing, delivery, and catalog copy.

The door clicked shut, and they sat down in full view of Tamara.

Practically spewing steam from both ears, she stalked to her desk, shut down the ancient laptop that chugged its way to slumber, and gathered her coat, bag, and soup.

The phone chirped. "Hey, get me a soy latte with a cinnamon twist," Nadine demanded. "Did you get those directions to the Hollywood Hills I asked you to give me because as usual they're not in front of me when I need them."

Tamara looked over her shoulder. Will sat hunkered down in one of the chairs facing Nadine's desk. She'd put them on her chair an hour ago.

"You're sitting on them." She vindictively stabbed the OFF button.

Why did Nadine have to be that way? When it was just the two of them, they were cool. But when Jesse, a client, or now Will stepped into the mix, she took up this mistress-maid thing that pissed her off.

Tamara headed out the door, weighing the consequences of not getting Nadine's soy latte so she could eat her dinner.

She then turned straight into the café, which was thankfully silent save for Dido playing over the sound system. In exactly forty-five minutes no seat would be left unclaimed when the after-work crowd arrived with a vengeance.

"She wants a soy latte and a cinnamon twist," Tamara announced when she came around the counter. Jesse peeked his head out of his tiny office.

"Does she want a shot of loogey?"

"Double shot." Tamara dumped her things on the battered couch they used as a catchall.

"She'll come over for it," he said when Tamara reached for her apron.

"And kill me."

"No she won't." His grin stretched as wide as the Cheshire cat. "Not if Will Benavides comes over to say hi."

She sneered at the silky way he pronounced his name.

"I have a question for you." Tamara abandoned the apron and sat on the stone hard arm of the couch. "Why does she put on this superiority act whenever someone else steps into the gallery?"

"Oh you noticed that, huh?"

"Uh-huh."

"Cynthia does that. I think she passed it to Nadine in the womb."

And why did Tamara ever think Jesse would give her a straight answer?

"Oh you are in a froth," he said, swiveling his chair around. "Look, when you have a mother like Cynthia, who is telling everyone around town that you'll be back at her door, asking for a job, it makes you put on this act that makes them think you're doing just fine. Understand?"

"I know, but should I call her on it?"

"Let me talk to her." His chair creaked as he leaned back. "Only family and her boyfriend who I'm not supposed to know about can talk to her about things like that."

Tamara ignored the juicy gossip bait he dangled in front of her nose.

"Thanks, Jesse." She uncapped her soup and dug the spoon out of her pocket. "You think I'm doing a good job, right?"

"Better than I thought."

"You're the one who told her to hire me."

"I was desperate."

Every part of Jesse, even his hair, brightened when Holly appeared in an eggplant-colored pantsuit and classic black leather boots. Tamara ate her soup while they hugged and kissed.

"You look tired," Jesse cooed. Tamara almost went, aww the way he tucked Holly into his chair. "Are you sure you want to work tonight?"

"I'll be fine as soon as I'm out of this thing." Stretching into a long yawn, Holly scruffed her fingers through her close-cropped hair. The dreads had been lopped off a few weeks ago. "Hey, Tamara, Will's out there. He asked for you."

The two of them delighted in this little turn of events like she'd just been asked to the prom. Carefully, she capped her soup and laid the spoon across the desk. She wouldn't give them the satisfaction of seeing her so much as glance in the mirror by the door.

She stepped out the door sensing exactly where he was but gave the café a slow scan to look as nonchalant as possible. But her pulse did a spirited jig when she saw him staring right at her, leaning across the counter.

"Hi," he said, when she approached.

She tensed, wanting him to kiss her, but then not wanting him to. She could imagine them leaning forward for a sweet kiss and Nadine bursting in the door demanding her soy latte.

"So you did it," Tamara said, stacking her hands on the counter. "Congratulations."

"Thanks. How've you been?"

Wondering why you didn't call, why I just didn't call, and whether or not I should get on the Pill. And how about you?

"Just working. You?"

"I took some extra shifts for my buddy and kept trying

to decide what I should do." He smiled, then looked down at his paint-smeared hands clasped into a tight ball.

"Can I see you sometime this weekend?" He asked so seriously that she felt just a twinge of sympathy for him.

"I have to work Saturday and go to my dad's birthday."

He straightened off the counter. "I have to work on Sunday. Maybe next time."

"You could come down with me Saturday night." She did a mental d'oh! But it was already out there like a fart on a first date.

"I don't want to get in the way if you're visiting your parents."

"It's my dad's birthday, so there'll be a ton of people there anyway." Give him an out. Quick. But dammit, she wanted to see him again.

She wanted to sit with him, ask more about him, and, of course, share one of those mind-bending kisses without Holly and Jesse pressing their ears to the wall behind her.

On the other hand, her dad's birthday might be a tragedy of epic proportions that would scar him for life.

"I don't have to wor—"

"If it's okay—" he started to say, then stopped. "Go ahead."

"You're more than welcome to come with me, but I don't have to work on Monday so if you want, we could meet up."

He studied her. The man definitely took his decisions quite seriously. "I'd like to see you on Saturday."

This might not be so bad, she thought. Will would act as the distraction, so everyone wouldn't just talk about her; they'd talk about what she was doing with him. Maybe after this he'd think she and her family were so nuts that she wouldn't have to worry about falling in love with him.

She smiled, hoping she didn't look like one of those Tim Burton aliens that chanted, "Do not run, we are your friends."

"Great," she said. "We'll need to be there at four."

20

"**TURN RIGHT HERE**," Tamara instructed Will, as he turned down her parents' street. "Oh my God, look at these trees. They're huge."

He glanced over at her, "You lived here right?"

"But I never really noticed them before." Lined on both sides of the smoothly paved street, the jacarandas were so old, and so thick they formed a canopy of green and lavender that carpeted the street with a lacy pattern of sunlight.

This was exactly the kind of neighborhood he'd imagined she would've grown up in.

"It's that house there." A banner decorated with balloons was strung across the walkway announcing, HAPPY 50TH JOHN.

This wasn't what he planned as what would technically be their first date. Actually they were breaking every rule in the dating world since he'd only seen her parents, having never been formally introduced to them. But he agreed and even went shopping for the casual, but not too casual, black pants and gray pullover sweater.

Tamara, as usual, looked so beautiful he nearly pushed her back upstairs into her apartment building. He didn't know how or why, but he just wanted to be with her all the time. And he wasn't going to push. Nor would he let go of any opportunity that came his way.

Will found a parking space two blocks down from her parents' house, killed the engine, and unsnapped his seat belt. Tamara sat so still, she seemed to have stopped breathing. Her fingers tightened around the edges of the pink box, filled with her mother's favorite pan dulce, that sat on her lap.

"Are you okay?" he asked. "I've got smelling salts in my med kit."

"You have a medical kit in your car?"

"And an OB/GYN kit, too."

"Why doesn't that surprise me?" she asked with a grin. "But I'll be fine, and—"

"And what?"

"Are you sure you want to do this because I just realized that this is way above and beyond what friends do for each other and when my family fights they really fight and my mother's friends, they'll probably ask you a million questions about us—"

He moved across the bench seat of his truck, sternly telling himself he wasn't going to kiss her. "If they ask, I'll tell them we're just sleeping together."

Her head whipped around, and he could tell for a second she really thought he was serious.

"You're supposed to laugh or at least crack a smile," he said, her perfume tempting him closer.

"If I was in the right frame of mind, I'd pay to see the looks on their faces if you said that."

"Look, I don't know how this whole thing works, but I'm sure your parents will be happy to see you. I'll be the distraction if things get intense."

"Like break a beer bottle over someone's head?"

He forced his eyes up from her lips. "Exactly." Well. Hell. He moved in and gave her the gentlest of kisses. So light he just brushed his lips over hers, warming his with her breath and the heat of her.

Will probably meant to distract her, and he damn well did. Except that what his kiss promised was not what a girl wanted lingering through her body as she visited her very angry parents.

He leaned back and grinned. "Let's go."

Agreeing, Tamara unsnapped her seat belt. They walked to the house without another word spoken between them until they reached the front door. Drawing in her breath and plastering a big smile on her face, she turned to him. "This is your chance to run like hell."

Will twisted the doorknob and opened the door. "Not without you."

They walked into the clamor of voices competing with Linda Ronstadt playing over the stereo.

Was there ever a Mexican family alive that didn't own that CD? she wondered with a shaky confidence.

"Tamara?" her dad asked, appearing in the hallway, wearing his orange-and-green apron.

"Happy birthday, Dad."

He pulled off his thick mitts as he approached, his eyes fastened on Will standing behind her. "I was wondering when you'd show up." He enveloped her in his arms, but she could feel his stare past her ear and her shoulder.

"Dad, this is Will Benavides. Will, this is my dad, John Contreras."

"*Mucho gusto,* Mr. Contreras."

"We've met before," her dad said. "You're Johnny's friend?"

"I am."

The only thing that seemed real in this very surreal moment as her dad and Will shook hands was the corner of the pastry box biting in the heel of her hand.

"Who's this clown?" Memo muttered, startling her when he hugged her.

"Be nice," Tamara warned her brother who lifted his chin and mad-dogged Will with an unwavering stare.

"Is that—?"

"Will Benavides. We went to high school together."

"What's he doing here?"

Isa appeared in the doorway of the kitchen. One glance at Will cornered up against the screen door and she sent Tamara a sly smile.

"What did you bring in the box?" Isa asked. She shoved Memo aside, destroying all credibility of his tough-guy act, and gave Tamara a hug.

"Mom's favorite pan dulce."

Isa whispered quickly, "She's in the kitchen and in a mood. She got into a fight with Yolanda this morning."

Oh great. Before Tamara could ask for details she heard her dad speak over the music. "Tamara never mentioned she was bringing a guest."

Isa took the pink box, gave it to Memo, and said, "Your mother needs you in the kitchen."

Tamara swept off to the rescue. "Did you get my gift?" She placed her hand on her dad's shoulder.

He turned and gave her the once-over. His eyebrows lifted in satisfaction at the dress and cashmere wrap Nadine had lent her after Jesse's lecture, and the new shoes she found on sale at a wholesale boutique in downtown. "Why are you all dressed up?"

She grinned, feeling a little small for wanting to appear like someone who didn't live in an apartment that overlooked defecating homeless people. "I . . . I just wanted to look nice."

The corner of his mouth quirked, "You look like you're one of those TV lawyers. Come in." He shouted to everyone. "Look who's here."

But everyone already knew. In seconds her mother's friends crowded around to get a good look at her and Will Benavides. Her dad pushed her down the hall, farther into the moist scent of simmering rice, corn tortillas, and the wonders of a thousand salads that crowded the dining room table.

Everyone's eyes widened with horrified delight as she was steered into the kitchen. The chatter died down so only Linda's ironclad voice filled the house.

"Susan, look who's here," her dad said, with an edge to his voice.

She turned around, holding the wooden spoon in her fist. Her eyes met Tamara's momentarily, then she flicked them away.

"Hello, Tamara," Tía Josie said. Her eyes darted from Tamara's mother and to her dad. "Was it a long drive down?"

"No, it was okay." Her dad squeezed her shoulders, and she could hear her heart pounding. "I brought your favorite sweet bread," Tamara said to her mother's back. "I thought you'd want it with your coffee tomorrow morning."

Without a word, her mother slammed a lid on one of the pots and stalked into the walk-in pantry.

"I'll just go . . ." Josie murmured after her mother.

Tamara felt everyone's stares crawling all over her, hungry for every detail of her humiliation.

Her dad patted the tops of her shoulders with both hands. "Come outside and help me with the barbecue." He leaned in so only she could hear. "I want to see what this Will person is all about."

Tamara stood before the door to her old bedroom.

She'd already endured three hours of conversations that generally started out with, "M'ija, who is this young man? When should we expect to be invited to the wedding?"

She'd had a few minutes to talk to Memo, who once again demonstrated discretion beyond his years and told her that Ruben slipped out the side yard. And she didn't even have a moment alone with Isa, who stuck to her mother's side.

But she understood. Isa had to live here, and, considering her problems with Yolanda, it was best that she stay with her mother. Still, it hurt that Isa didn't slip in beside her, and ask, "So? When were you planning to tell me?"

But she had to talk to her mother before she went home.

Face-to-face. Her breath shook as she lifted her fist to knock, then snatched it back. What would she say? Maybe she should think about this because chances are she'd say the wrong thing, and her mom would get all pissed off again.

Oh hell. What else could she possibly do that would make her mom even angrier than she already was?

Drawing her shoulders back, she tapped her fingers on the door. "Mom, I'm going back now," she called through the door.

No response.

"Can I come in?" She debated if she should knock again. "I just wanted to say good night."

Canned laughter from the TV in the living room mocked her.

"I really liked your potato salad this time," she said. "It was different from the way you always—"

Tamara flinched when the door swung back.

"—the way you always make it," she finished.

Now that they stood face-to-face, the words scurried into some hidden compartment in her mind.

Her mother held on to the doorknob with one hand, pressing a paperback Tamara left behind to her chest. Staring at Tamara's chin, she kept her mouth in a sullen line.

"Wow, it really looks nice in here." She peeked inside. Her brief glimpse captured the warm glow of a reading lamp poised over a daybed covered with a rose-patterned quilt. "You finally got your own room."

Still nothing.

"Do you like that book? Suzanne Brockmann . . . uh . . . she's a really cool writer and you can never guess what'll happen and . . ."

"Is there something you want?"

Tamara held out the invitation that she and Nadine put together the previous day. She had considered giving it to her dad, but thought maybe it would be a gesture to her mom that all she wanted was to get her back.

"I wanted to invite you to the art show I've been working on." She wished her mother would at least look at her. "We're having a reception. All the artists will be there and Will's paintings will be there and—"

"Give it to your father," her mother said crisply, retreating into the room.

"Mom, wait." The invitation trembled between them. "Can we please get this behind us?"

"I have nothing to say—"

"I'm applying to graduate school," she interrupted. "I finished my applications, and one of the schools I want to go to is in San Francisco."

Tamara waited a moment. "I'm not sure if San Francisco is really right for me. So I thought I'd talk to you and see what you thought."

"I don't care what you do," her mother said thickly.

"But I . . . I just want to know why you . . . why we can't talk anymore? Dad isn't mad at me anymore, and you always said that there's nothing we couldn't ever talk about, so I ju—"

"You're an embarrassment to me and your father," she said matter-of-factly. "Do you know how long we've had to deal with people's questions? The rumors? And now you bring this man into our home when you haven't been broken up with Ruben for even a month."

"We broke up in June."

"Don't interrupt me," she thundered. "I didn't raise you to act *como una sucia*. And here you are, flaunting him in front of all of us like you don't care what people will think. You're only making a fool of yourself."

"But I—" was all that she got in before the door slammed shut in her face. Pulse drumming, she turned, and her gaze snagged on Will, who stood in the mouth of the hallway.

"You want to go home?" he asked after they'd stared at each other.

She shut her eyes, just imagining how much Will had heard. What the hell had she just done? She'd just dragged this incredible guy into all this mess. This had to be the stupidest stunt she'd ever pulled.

"If you want me to, I can just take you straight home and we can do this some other time," he said. "Or if you'd rather stay and—"

Opening her eyes, Tamara said, "No. Let's go."

She walked quickly past him so he wouldn't try to comfort her or do something that would make her burst into tears. After Tamara said her good-byes to her dad and Memo from within a fog, she went home with Will, realizing that she'd really lost her mother.

21

"**A**RE YOU SURE you want me to come up?" Will asked when Tamara drew the elevator gates shut.

"I have a book I meant to give you," she said.

Tamara hadn't said much on the way back. When she had walked out of the hallway she'd lost most of her color and held herself like her whole body ached.

He figured whatever happened between her and her mom wasn't good. He wanted to do something, say something that would bring her back.

"I could come back tomorrow." God, what was he saying? "But since we're here . . ."

Her finger hovered over the fourth-floor button. "I'm so sorry you had to hear all of that. I don't know what I was thinking—"

Her thin shoulders jerked up then down like she was trying not to cry. Will wanted to take her in his arms and hold her until . . . until what?

Even though Mrs. Contreras ignored him, and her

brother, Memo, gave him the evil eye, Will actually liked being there. There was some complicated reason Johnny wasn't there that Tamara couldn't exactly explain, but Will still enjoyed himself. He liked walking through the house she'd grown up in and looking across the party at her, knowing he'd come with her.

"Like I said before, I don't know how all this family stuff works, but I'm sure you'll work it out," he said. Tamara held herself still when he touched the soft underside of her arm. That was one big signal telling him she needed to be alone.

If she was someone else, he wouldn't be standing here feeling helpless yet wanting to do or say something that would make her feel better.

But he'd been yearning for her since that day they had lunch, when she let him hold and kiss her on the street.

Will backed off, letting his hand fall away. He wasn't screwing this up, even if the wait killed him.

She opened the elevator door, and they walked down a hall straight out of a Raymond Chandler novel.

Will was so busy figuring out how he was going to say good night that it took him a moment to realize that she'd opened the door to her apartment.

"Have a seat," she said so softly that he wouldn't have known what she meant if she hadn't pointed to the futon.

Will decided he'd stay for a moment, then go straight to his cold shower at home.

Her place was about as big as his living room. No, he thought as he looked around, much smaller. She escaped behind a thin door and flipped on the light.

He looked for a TV, more furniture. Instead the walls

were decorated with Picasso prints and a painting of a mermaid holding on to the stem of a water lily. A tiny table stood in front of the window with a purple glass vase. A pink bookcase stuffed with books stood next to the closet door, and Chinese paper lanterns she'd hung from ceiling hooks glowed in the tiny room.

His eyebrows rose when he noticed that she'd stuck sticky notes with Spanish words written on them on just about everything in her apartment.

Tamara came out of the bathroom.

"How long have you lived here?" he asked, his eyes following her to a card table squashed in the tiny kitchen.

"As long as I've worked for Nadine. I wouldn't look out the windows if I were you."

Will twisted around. "Why?"

She made that funny grin she made when she was embarrassed. "It's the local bathroom for the homeless."

Will didn't say anything for a moment as he just watched her intently. "Did I make things worse for you with your mom?"

"No, why?"

"She was giving me the evil eye."

She sat on the futon next to him, holding out a book on Edward Hopper. He resisted the urge to touch even her hand.

"I really am sorry about tonight," she said, straightening to face him. "I imagine you heard everything she said, and I don't want you to think any of it was because of you. She's probably mad at me because I wasn't there last night and this morning helping."

He jumped in when she paused for breath. "That's cool."

Intending to leave like a gentleman, his hands slapped the tops of his thighs and he moved to stand. But he made the fatal mistake of looking her straight in the eyes.

"What's happening here, Tamara?" he asked.

Normally Tamara would've played dumb to keep the distance between them. But from the very beginning lying and game playing just didn't feel right between them. "I don't know."

"But you know something's going on between us, right?"

This wasn't the right time for this, not when her family was so screwed up, and she had plans that didn't exactly include him. He was a fantasy come true, and what if he wanted more from her and she couldn't . . .

"Tamara," he murmured, bringing her back to the present.

"I don't know, it's like you came out of nowhere and I . . ." She lost her courage and sank down into the futon.

"Do you want me to go?"

She did, and she didn't. He took in a deep breath, then let it go.

How could she be so sure about this? What if she fell in love with him? What if she couldn't stay in L.A.? Could she walk away from him?

In spite of the doubts that gnawed on the corners of her mind, Tamara slipped across the futon for a kiss.

He bent forward, still keeping his eyes on hers, to meet her.

She inhaled sharply, piercing her senses with the scent and the taste of him. The hot feel of his hands through the material of her dress as they traveled up her back and into her hair made her wet and twitching. She fisted her hands full of his shirt as she mashed her body against his, wanting him on her, in her, even though she didn't know where falling for him would lead her.

Will was an enigma. He made her laugh, he never told her to get to the point, and if he could do this to her by just touching her back . . . she forgot what her point was when he swept his tongue into her mouth.

But he slowed down, easing the pressure of his hands and the ferocity of his kiss.

"Tamara," he begged against the corner of her mouth. "We better stop now."

He scraped her cheek with his rough one, planting small kisses on her temple, her ear. Tamara closed her eyes and licked her lips as she rested her forehead on his shoulder. She heard the unspoken "but I won't unless you want me to" in his silence.

Should she? Her body screamed, *Hell, yes;* but her mind cautioned, *Hold on there, sister.*

"I'm not sorry for that, are you?" he finally said. She felt his grin.

"No," she whispered.

"I'll go." He squeezed her closer. "And we can take up where we left off later."

She forced herself to look him in the eye when he peeled himself apart from her. "Are you okay with that?" he asked, gently tipping up her chin.

"No."

His frown reappeared.

"I want you to stay with me."

"Are you sure?"

God, was he for real? "No . . . I'm making it up."

He bent to kiss her again and his eyes flicked up. "Did you know the people in the other building can see us?"

With that delirious pressure bearing down between her legs, Tamara hardly cared about curtains. She sprang up and in four strides slapped off the lights, then was back straddling his lap.

The pale darkness allowed him to see her as they kissed. He hoisted her up and twisted so he'd be on top.

"Please tell me you have condoms," she whispered, then drew his earlobe between her teeth.

"Yeah," he groaned. "Got it."

Abruptly he lifted himself off her, kneeling between her legs. She stared up at him, her hair spread like seaweed around her head.

Enjoying her watching him, he unbuttoned his shirt enough so he could yank it over his head. He grinned down at her as her eyes wildly explored him.

"You can touch me," he whispered.

She smiled as she pressed her hand over his right nipple. "You usually talk to me in Spanish," she whispered.

He got the button on his pants undone, then hesitated. "No I don't."

She scooted back and sat up to run both hands over his naked skin. "I don't know what you're saying, but it sounds beautiful."

He sucked in his breath when she kissed the center of his chest.

She rubbed her cheek against him, "You smell so good."

If he didn't get his pants off immediately, there'd be no

way he'd be able to work his zipper. "Tamara, wait a minute—"

Her wicked hands slid down past the waist of his pants. Their eyes linked. Her lips curled, and his mouth fell open as her hand pressed harder and harder over him.

"Show me," she said, leaning back on her elbows.

The zipper burred as he eased it down. Tamara wouldn't stop staring him in the eye, even as he pushed his pants down his legs. Unable to stop himself, he let himself kiss her again.

Kissing never felt so complete. As much as he ached to bury himself deep inside her, he never experienced anything as exciting as the way their mouths and tongues made love. With others it'd just been a necessary step. An enjoyable one, but one that never felt like this.

His hips began rocking over her, feeling her dress work its way up to her waist.

Too rushed to explain, he yanked off his briefs. She stood up off the bed, wrestling the zipper down the side of her dress. All she wore underneath were grape-colored panties and a bra that clasped in the front.

"*Quieras a besar aqui,*" he said, sliding his fingers between the clasp.

She moved her hands to cover herself when it gave way. "Don't," he asked. "I want to taste you."

"I nev—" Will's fingers brushing over her nipples jolted her protest to a halt.

"Never what?" he asked, pressing her against him so her belly and the tops of her thighs touched his hot skin.

This wasn't the time to tell him about her boring sex life, so she kept quiet.

As he drew her into his mouth his fingers slid her panties down her hips. She made some unintelligible sound, and her chin dropped into his hair. He released her so she could stand and step out of them.

"Come here," he whispered, making room for her to lie down beside him. He took her hand, holding it against his solid chest, then moved it over his flat stomach, the hair that started below his belly button, then *down there*.

"Oh, you mean this?" she teased, wrapping her fingers around him.

He groaned, letting her see by the way his eyes widened and then squeezed shut, what her hand did to him.

She tightened her grip and moved her hand faster, loving that his hips jerked in time to her stroking.

"Tamara, stop. You've gotta stop." He grabbed her hand and rolled on top of her. Every nerve in her body screamed.

"Will," she cried, her hands seeking purchase and finding the bars of the futon.

She'd never been more excited by the sound of ripping plastic than at that moment. Tamara opened her eyes to see him kneeling over her, his hands holding her knees wide apart.

"Look at me, Tamara," he said, his eyes wild and desperate for her.

He eased himself into her. He took her carefully, almost as if this was her first time. His breath hissed when they were fully joined, and for a second he didn't move.

"I'm not hurting you, am I?"

"No," she whispered, finding his hand with hers. Their fingers threaded together. He began sliding in and out of her, making both of them lose any awareness of an outside world, of breath, and of time.

He adjusted the angle at which he took her, and for the first time control was yanked from her grasp. She clasped her thighs around his waist and felt every nerve in her body catch fire.

His skin slapped furiously against hers until he froze above her, his face a tight mask of pleasure and pain as he moaned her name.

Afterward, she held him, following the path of his spine with her fingers and back up. Their breaths slowed and evened, and her eyelids grew heavy.

"I'm sorry if that was so quick," he murmured. He hoisted himself up to sit on the edge of the futon.

"It was worth every second," she whispered.

He smiled down at her over his shoulder. "So I get to stay the night?"

"Don't ask dumb questions." She rose up to kiss him again.

"CAN I COME OUT?"

Will heard Tamara laugh from the futon where he left her.

"Hold on," she called. He heard her hiss, then two hopping footsteps on the wood floor; two more and the futon bounced. "Okay, they're gone."

Even though he'd put his briefs on sometime around four in the morning, he didn't want strangers seeing him through the window. He flopped down beside her, and she yanked the covers over them. She lay on her side facing him, with that big gorgeous smile he loved.

Last night they hadn't slept much, but sleep was the last thing he wanted. He felt alive, shit, giddy having spent the whole night talking in the dark while playing with her hand. They'd made love twice, the second time slowly, with lots of kissing and touching.

He'd tried teaching her how to speak to him in Spanish, but she'd gotten embarrassed.

Last night was the best night of his sorry-assed life and

as the apartment filled with the late-morning sunlight, he never wanted to leave the little world they'd made between them.

She snuggled up to him so they were almost nose to nose.

He'd never been comfortable being physical with a woman beyond the obligatory cuddling after gettin' down. But with her he felt completely natural.

"I'm on days off for the next couple of days," he said, running his finger down her cheek.

"Yeah?"

"Uh-huh. So I was thinking that you might want to stay with me at my place."

"What about Señora Allende?"

"She leaves tonight to spend her week with her daughters."

Tamara took a deep breath. "I have some applications I wanted to work on."

"Bring them. You can use my computer."

"What are you going to do?"

"Work on a new canvas I started the other day."

"You don't mind me hanging around?"

Will shook his head.

"What about the one you showed me the other day. Did you finish it?"

He didn't want his time with her tainted in any way by his mother or brother. He didn't want bad memories lingering in the back of his head while he had her.

"I started a new one. I'm stuck on the other one, so I'll put it away for later."

Will saw the questions in her eyes; damn, she had the

most expressive eyes. "You applying to USC again?" he asked.

She nodded, her hair whispering against the pillow. "And two more schools."

"Where?"

"Cal State Long Beach and San Francisco State."

"San Francisco?"

The questions were gone. Replaced by something else.

They were quiet for a moment. The sheets whispered as she sat up. She'd put on a tank top and some faded bottoms with little cars all over them.

"I know this is kind of awkward, but I'm in a real um . . . unsettled place in my life and—" She caught him grinning at her. "What?"

"I understand." He did. But he wasn't going to let it show, *it* being the hollowness he'd lived with for so long that he no longer wanted now that he had her.

"Are you sure?"

"I know enough about you to understand how much you want that degree." He sat up, resting his weight on his elbow. "But it's 'SC you really want, right?"

"There's a real big chance I won't get in. The current class has only three women."

But there was Cal State Long Beach. And maybe he could do some checking on his own to see if there were other programs in smaller schools in L.A.

"When will you find out if you get accepted?"

"Same time as the last time. Late May or June."

"So it's October now . . ." He counted off the months with the fingers of his free hand. "We have about seven months."

Tamara's gaze fell to the sheets, as she played with the edge of her blanket. "What are you trying to ask me?"

His heart leapt, then ran at full speed. This was what he thought he'd never have. And it seemed like he hadn't even been looking when wham! Here they were, sitting in bed after making love and talking and laughing in the dark like they'd been together forever.

"Are you okay with us being together exclusively?"

Her smile won over the surprise, and she looked back up at him when he took her left hand, systematically kissing each knuckle. "I feel like we're in high school again," she said.

"I didn't get a chance to ask you out in high school."

"Would you have?"

He nipped her thumb. "Maybe."

"Only maybe?"

Will tugged her hand but she stayed firm.

"Okay, yes, I would've. But would you have said yes?"

She nodded, answering that one question that haunted him ever since he last saw her after his graduation.

"So, Tamara, will you be my girlfriend?" he asked in a husky, dork voice.

"Yes," she answered back. He tugged her again, and she tugged back.

Well, if she wouldn't come to him, then he'd just have to go to her. "But you're not upset that it took this long for me to ask?"

"The people across the way can see us," she whispered, as he levered his body over her, nudging her onto her back.

"Not if we stay on this side of the bed."

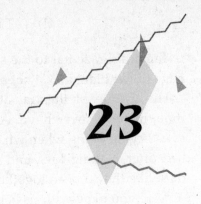

23

WHAT WAS THAT Will person doing with Tamara?

Oh, Susan had heard the stories about him. Tattooing his classmates under the football bleachers, slightly above average grades, and the foster family that let him run wild.

Even Isa hadn't known Tamara was dating him.

"Forget about it," she muttered to herself.

She told herself not to care or ask questions about what Tamara did.

And he seemed like a nice boy. John said little except that he was a fireman, and he didn't like the way Will looked at her the couple of times he'd caught him.

"Like how?" she'd asked.

"The way I'd look at you."

Just thinking about the way John had said it made Susan stand up from her computer desk.

Her nerves wouldn't settle down. Her eyes would close at night, but sleep came reluctantly. Ever since that night, after the party she wondered, *Could it be true?*

Shaking her head, she sat with a bounce on the love seat. She opened her book but didn't see the pages when she remembered Tamara had taken their old answering machine.

It wasn't any of her business as she stared at the phone.

Only this once. Just to see if it were possible that her daughter was carrying on with this Will.

She made sure the door was closed. John's football game played in the living room. It was nearly seven on Monday. Susan had overheard Memo telling John that she sometimes worked at the café Monday nights. She picked up the phone and dialed Tamara's number. She gripped the receiver when Tamara's voice spoke back to her.

I'm her mother, she reasoned with the tightness in her neck. *Even if she doesn't want me as hers.*

Before the greeting ended, Susan punched in the old pass code to give her access to the messages this Will person might have left on the machine.

"Who are you talking to?"

"Ay!" She jerked both feet off the ground, holding the phone to her racing heart.

John stood in the doorway, holding her office door open. His eyebrows winged up, and his eyes lingered on the phone.

"I was leaving Josie a message," she lied, punching the OFF button.

"Then why didn't you leave it?"

"Why don't you knock?" She tossed the evidence of her guilt on the love seat. "You could've killed me!"

He leaned his shoulder on the doorframe. "Did you see this?"

She recognized the invitation Tamara tried to give her Saturday. Taking in a deep breath, she reminded herself that she was perfectly justified in what she'd told Tamara.

"No," she answered.

"It's for Tamara's gallery party. Do you want to go?"

"Absolutely not."

A tortured sigh followed by pursed lips made her shoulders pull back.

"Susanna, when are you going to get over this? She's our daughter."

"Not mine."

"Since when? Since she finally cut off those apron strings you had tied around her neck?"

She gasped. Of all people, her own husband would say such things—

"I wasn't happy with the way she went about things, but she's an adult, and we always said we wouldn't be the parents who stopped our girl from living her own life. Remember?" She heard the accusations in his voice that it was her fault they no longer ate Sunday dinner as a family.

"How dare you? Stand there like it didn't hurt you when she announced she'd sold the car we'd bought for her college graduation and just upped and left. Don't put all the blame on me."

"No one is blaming you, mujer. But I will if you don't come with us. It's time to end all this foolishness and be a family again."

She'd had enough.

"Out of my room." She came at him, ready to bodily shove him out if that's what it took. "I've had enough of you."

"*¡Basta!*"

She'd nearly flipped backward she stopped so fast. John had only shouted at her a handful of times in the twenty-seven years they had been married.

Why was he treating her like this? Tears stung her eyes, not recognizing the furious man in front of her.

"You want to mope around in here, fine," he yelled. "I'm tired of all of this."

The window blinds shuddered at the force with which he slammed the door.

Susan held her hand out as she sank onto the edge of the love seat. She stared at the invitation she'd ripped in half and thrown into the trash can.

SHE'S THIS CLOSE to drowning herself in the fountain."

Tamara looked up from the list of reserved guests to Jesse wringing his hands in the doorway of Nadine's office. Veins tensed in his forehead, and his eyes looked like they were going to shoot out of his head.

"What?"

"She's threatening to leave."

"Why?"

Jesse's pale hands brushed the front of his boxy black coat. "Cynthia called."

Dread raced down the back of her neck. "When?" She started for the hallway.

"I don't know, twenty minutes ago." He stayed close on her heels. "Where are you going? What are you going to say?"

"I don't know," she said calmly. But this could take a while. "Find the red dots in the storage cabinet and remind the caterer to move the heat lamps from the garden to the front."

Tamara flattened against the wall when the bartender sped down the hallway with a case of wine.

"Where do you want me to put the red dots?" Jesse asked.

"By my phone."

Jesse sputtered behind her. "But I have media coming here tonight, and I need to be—"

She did an abrupt 180 turn. "Would you rather fish Nadine out of the fountain?"

If she hadn't been so close to bursting into shrapnel from the stress, Tamara would've laughed at the way Jesse's eyes blinked like a faulty neon sign.

"Go talk to her," he insisted, waving her down the hall. "I'll round up one of the caterers."

All Tamara had left was fifty-six minutes to pull Nadine out of her psychodrama, make sure caterers moved the heat lamps as she had asked them to an hour ago, then change out of her jeans and stretched-out sweater before the opening officially began.

Then Will turned the corner.

She took in a rib-splitting breath. She had to do something about those fingers of anticipation that tickled her insides whenever she saw him.

"When did you get here?"

He grinned, holding his jacket, still on its hanger, over his shoulder. "You were yelling at the alcohol guy when I walked in. Hi." He kissed her. "Want to step outside with me?" he asked.

She sighed for lost opportunities. "Nadine's threatening to leave. Her mother is boycotting the event."

"Have you heard anything from your mom?"

"My dad, Memo, and Isa are coming."

"Will you be okay?"

She hitched one shoulder. She'd been deliberately too busy to really think about it. "What am I going to do?"

He kissed her forehead.

"Did you invite Jones?"

"He's on duty tonight."

"That's too bad, I bet he would've . . ."

She sensed that wall creep up between them as he straightened away from her. Family and friends, except for Señora Allende and the group they'd formed with Nadine, Jesse, Holly, and the rest of them, were out of bounds with him.

"Umm . . . would've liked to see your stuff," she finished.

He tucked a piece of hair behind her ear, then caressed her face. "You better get out there."

You've got it bad, Isa's words repeated themselves as they so often did ever since Tamara gave her the skinny on Will.

"See you later?" he asked.

"Of course."

So what if she was at the point where she missed him on the nights he was on duty and knew why he so passionately hated chocolate?

Tamara yanked open the back door, stiffening when the eastbound wind slapped her in the face. Glancing up, she hoped it wouldn't start to rain until after the reception.

Sitting at the far end of the narrow garden space between the two freight buildings, Nadine hugged herself against the gray cold.

"It's cold out here," Tamara said.

"I know."

Tamara spied the crumpled cigarette pack rocking to the rhythm of the wind on the iron table. She didn't want to contribute to Nadine's sure death of lung cancer, but if nicotine was the only thing that would pull her out of a mother-induced funk, Tamara had no shame in running next door for more.

She sat on the ledge of the silent fountain. "What's going on?"

"Nothing." Nadine pushed her glasses up the bridge of her nose. "Why aren't you wearing a jacket?"

"I left it inside." Tamara stretched for something else to say. "The gallery looks beautiful."

"I should just cancel the whole thing."

"I even cleaned your desk," Tamara ignored her. "Did you know that you have a message slip dating from February 2002?"

Nadine curled her lips. "I hate these things."

Tamara didn't ask if she meant pink message slips.

"I don't know why I just didn't stay where I was." Nadine straightened, tucking her hands between her legs. "Why did I even bother?"

For the first time ever, Tamara saw Nadine look defeated. "Do you know that's all she kept saying on the phone?" Nadine suddenly asked.

"For the fucking millionth time she asked why I sold the Santa Monica town house and cashed out my savings when I could've kept working for her? I mean tonight of all nights she has to bring that up again?"

Tamara managed to keep up with Nadine's reference to her mother.

"Then when I tell her that I can't go back and change things and get the hell off my back, she starts on this guilt trip that maybe she won't come if she makes me so upset."

With a huff she sat back in the iron chair, fisting her fingers into her hair. "I can never fucking win with her."

When she was sure the storm had passed, Tamara ventured forth, "I don't think we're supposed to win with our mothers. I think we're here to take their crap, then heap it on our own kids."

Nadine's lips curled. "You're a real help."

Tamara shrugged, suspicious of the sprinkles that dotted the tabletop. "At least you talk to your mother. Mine won't even return my calls."

"Still?"

Rubbing the little hairs that stood on end all over her arms, she decided to change the subject. "Jesse confirmed that the writer from the *L.A. Times* is coming, and that guy who freelances for *American Art Magazine* is also coming."

"Do you think she'll come tonight?" Nadine persisted.

"I doubt it."

"At least you'll have Will to comfort you."

Tamara pretended not to hear that. "I have to check on the caterer and see when they're planning to move the heaters to the front."

"Oh don't play that shit with me," Nadine said, coming back to life. " 'Fess up. He was all over you the other day."

And the other night, Tamara remembered, but kept that to herself. "Oh, just so you know," she continued, "the caterer brought the second case of white wine."

Then her mind quickly switched tracks. "And no he

wasn't. He was too busy refereeing you and Jesse installing his paintings."

"He's a good guy," Nadine declared. "Why try to hide it?"

"We're not hiding—" Tamara bit her bottom lip. "What if I don't get accepted to a school in L.A.?"

"How the hell am I supposed to know?"

Tamara should've got the damn cigarettes.

"While you're agonizing over it, I'm going inside." The cigarette pack crackled as it disappeared in Nadine's pale fist.

This was all screwed up. Will was supposed to be a fantasy come true, their affair something she'd remember fondly when she was eighty. He wasn't supposed to be the guy she'd fallen in love with.

Tamara looked up and blinked against dots of rain carried away by the brisk winds that hustled streaks of white clouds. The rain had done such a good job of cleaning up the city that stars twinkled sleepily in the primrose sky. "I don't know what I'll do," she said.

"Well it's not like you have to decide now." Nadine's boot crunched against the brick, still dark with old rain. "Come on. Nothing like a little chaos to shut up a case of the what-ifs."

"Well I'm glad to have cheered you up."

"So am I," Nadine said, putting her arm over Tamara's shoulders. "You're good for that."

25

"INEVER LIKED the way you did my nose," Señora Allende declared, standing arm in arm with Will in front of what she declared, *her painting.* "It's too big."

"You're making that up," he replied.

"No. From this angle, *es muy gigante.*"

He hitched the corner of his mouth as she patted his arm. "It's sold. So if you tell the new owner, you'll cost me a sale."

She considered that. "You will paint me again. *Con mis rosas.*"

With his free hand, Will reached for her hand and squeezed it. "I can do that."

In unison they walked to the next canvas, *his* canvas, which gleamed under the studio lights overhead.

Unlike that first night he'd walked in this gallery, Will now belonged. And knowing that Tamara was here with him, that she would go home with him, made him feel like Fate looked into his dreams and made them real.

He caught more than a few eyes following him through the gallery, which glowed with the light of thick white candles burning in wrought-iron stands.

Two flamenco guitarists thrummed *"Como Fue"* in the center of the room.

The candles made the fireman in him nervous, but he appreciated the romance and mystery they created, especially when he stole those precious ten seconds with Tamara in the hallway.

"Ay, m'ijo," Señora Allende sighed. "This feels good."

He grinned down at her.

"For a minute there you had me thinking I'd never get to see something like this."

"Neither did I," he admitted. "Thank you."

She nodded. "I only want happiness for you."

He wondered if he should say anything. "I'm telling her about the painting."

Knowing which painting he meant, the one he'd secretly worked on the few nights he didn't spend with Tamara, Señora Allende pressed his arm harder against her side. "Are you sure?"

"Yeah."

"Everything? Don't tell her half the story, m'ijo. Tell her everything or else you will never be able to truly start your life together."

It happened so fast, barely a month since she showed up that afternoon when he was mowing the lawn. She had his heart, and now he'd give her his secrets. Will took in a deep breath. "I know."

She patted his hand with hers. *"Donde no hay amor, no hay dolor. ¿Entiendes?"*

Where there is no love, there is no pain. Will answered with a nod.

She seemed satisfied, but then drew her eyebrows together in a frown. "How come this one hasn't sold?"

The tension passed, and he let himself joke with her. "I don't know."

A quick perusal, and she pulled her arm free to plant both fists on her hips. "There's nothing wrong with it."

"All the others sold," he reminded her.

Not good enough, he could almost hear her thinking. But then her frown softened, her lips rolled out of that prim line, and for an unguarded moment, her whole self seemed to deflate.

"What?" he asked. "Are you okay?"

"Fine, fine," she dismissed, pulling her shoulders back.

He let out an exasperated breath. She'd been playing this ever since he ripped her bathroom floor apart. But every time he let her off the hook.

"Come on, I saw it. What's up?"

Señora Allende glanced up at him, then back at the painting. Quiet for a moment, the party hummed between and around them while he waited for her answer.

She wet her murderous red lips then said, "I'm putting the house for sale, m'ijo. I found a nice young lady who sold her abuela's house last month. You know that one on the hill with the eucalyptus trees?"

"Yeah. You made me fix her door."

"Sí." She lifted her chin, determined not to show the fear, the anguish he'd already seen. "Did you know she got $150,000 for that house?" She pulled herself up a little straighter. "And she never did a thing to it."

"That's good," he said, playing along.

"I should get at least $200,000."

"Maybe you can take a cruise like you always wanted to."

Lifting her eyebrows, she looked up at him. *"Tal vez."*

Will turned around when he felt a long-nailed finger tap his shoulder.

"Hey, Nadine," he drawled when he turned to her and her grandma beaming up at him. "Señora Villaseñor."

Will gave Señora Allende a look that warned they'd talk about this later. She narrowed her eyes for him to mind his own business.

"We're very proud of you, m'ijo," Doña Villaseñor said. He had to bend down for her to hug and give him a kiss on the cheek.

"Señora Allende," Nadine said, reaching for her hand. "I have something to show both of you."

Nadine held out her wineglass for Will to hold. She peeled off a red sticker and stuck it on the white card bearing his name and the title of his canvas, *Exposition and Vermont.*

"Congratulations." She took her glass back. "How does it feel to have one less painting in your garage?"

Like he'd just sold his right foot. He was going to miss that little girl crossing the empty lot glittering with broken glass.

"When do I get my check?" he asked with a lopsided grin.

Nadine turned to Señora Allende. "His sentimental side kills me. How do you put up with him?"

While they talked about him, he glanced around the packed gallery for Tamara. Even in heels and a powerful black suit with pink pinstripes, she still got lost in a crowd.

"She's busy hostessing," Nadine answered. He turned and saw the three of them grinning.

"Matilda, it's time for us to go," Doña Villaseñor said, her eyes twinkling with that knowing glitter.

"*Ah, sí,*" Señora Allende returned. She embraced Will. "*Buenas noches, m'ijo.* And tell Tamara I said good night."

"I will," he said. "Thank you again."

She brushed the sleeve of his shirt and squeezed his chin before she walked away with Señora Villaseñor. There's no way he would've let her get in a car with her comadre behind the wheel. But Nadine hired a town car to drive them, and the chauffeur waited by the door in a black suit and red tie.

"He's cute," Nadine said, her eyes lingering across the room before taking her wineglass back. "So what do you think?"

"He's not my type."

She wrinkled her nose at him, then sipped from her wine. "I meant, what do you think about our Tamara possibly moving to San Francisco?"

Hearing it felt like a knife tearing through his chest. He knew it was a possibility; he just chose to ignore it.

"She should do what's best for her," he said evenly, keeping his eyes locked with Nadine's.

She didn't hide the grin that touched her lips. Leaning forward, "Between you and me, we need to stick together to keep her here."

He found his tongue. "Only if that's what she wants."

Her eyes narrowed behind her glasses. "Don't go too far. I want you to meet someone."

With a satisfied look, she sailed off. Will scanned the

room again, grinding his cocktail napkin in his fist. He found Tamara in the front corner of the gallery smiling and nodding at some blond guy in a casual suit who stood too close, with a cheeky smile and a glass of red wine in his hand.

Will took a step forward toward the shifting, laughing crowd.

Tamara looked his way as if she sensed him approaching, and her whole face broke into that smile.

"Hello, you," she said with a secret glint in her eye that reminded him of the last time he kissed her. "This gentleman was just asking about your work."

While she introduced them—Will didn't quite catch his name—the blond guy did the math.

That's right, pretty boy, Will threatened silently, *she's mine.*

"I better say hello to Nadine," blond guy conceded, offering his hand. Will squeezed just enough to make his point. "I've heard your collection is nearly sold out."

"That's what I heard," Will said.

Tamara lightly smacked his arm when the dumb-ass left. "What was all that about?"

"We need to talk." Will stepped in front of her, blocking them from the rest of the party.

"Okay, but can it wait until this is over?"

The words "San Francisco" jumped up and down on the tip of his tongue, insisting to be let out. But Will held back. He knew he had to approach this one carefully. They never really talked about a future together, and he didn't want to do it here of all places.

"We're going to your place after this, right?" he asked.

The start of a sexy smile started. "Of course. But I have to stay until the caterers are finished."

"I'll wait."

For some stupid reason he was suddenly feeling the need to stop circling around her and put himself and his feelings on the line. Just tell her that even though he'd wanted her from the very first moment they'd met, he'd found that the real her was a helluva lot better than the fantasy of her he'd carried around until now.

"Tamara, I—"

Out of the corner of her eye she saw Isa walk in first, then her dad, and finally Memo. The rest of what Will said swooped up in a vacuum. Tamara drew in her breath, hoping her mother would walk in next.

But she didn't.

"I'm sorry," she said absently. "My . . . they just walked in."

The three of them looked around like they'd landed on another planet.

She knew deep down that her mother wouldn't come. And so it shouldn't have hurt, as she nudged and shuffled her way to them.

"Hi, guys," she said brightly.

Her dad smiled. He moved his arms as if to hug her, then looked around. "This is very fancy."

She hugged him anyway. "It could be worse. But thanks."

Memo hugged her next. "Is that clown here tonight?"

Before she could punch his arm, Isa nudged him aside. "This is so cool," she said. "Did you set this all up by yourself?" Tamara had a second to admire the way she wore her hair swept up off the back of her neck before they embraced. She had also lost some weight, and there were the faint beginnings of circles under her eyes.

But she looked strong.

"Only some of it."

Now came the awkward part, as she faced her dad. He saw the disappointment she fought so hard to hide.

"Memo, go get me a soda," he said.

Memo's eyes were glued to a bronze nude female torso that arched and twisted skyward.

"We're going to get something to drink," Isa insisted, herding him off.

Tamara's dad stuffed his hands in what he called his "nice pants." She put a little more muscle into her smile, feeling cold in spite of the heat of so many bodies pressed into a tight space.

"Your mother couldn't make it tonight," he said. "She wasn't feeling well."

"That's okay. It was raining, and she never liked being out late anyway," she said. "Was it raining down in Sweetwater?"

Dreading the awkward silence or even worse, the more awkward explanations, Tamara gestured him deeper into the gallery. "Come in and see the collection. We already sold a third of the paintings."

"Where's your friend?"

Confused, Tamara tilted her head to the side.

"Will." A smile tickled the corners of his mouth.

"Oh. He's around."

"Is he going to say hello to me?"

"Yeah. But he's busy right now."

Her dad remained silent.

"His paintings are over there," she said. "They're nearly sold out."

Still nothing.

Getting itchy, she crossed her arms over her chest. "What?"

"So how serious is it with you two?"

Tamara spotted Will standing with a gentle-looking lady in a pink suit and pearls in front of the canvas with the little girl. Nadine caught Tamara looking and winked. The camera flashed, then Will bent closer to listen what his new patron said.

There had to be a way she could avoid his question. Wonder Woman would know.

Will walked, God, toward them.

"Hi," she said, feeling short of breath when he looked at her then her dad. "You remember my dad."

"Mr. Contreras." He held out his hand, and her dad waited just a second too long to take it.

"Congratulations."

"They're over on that wall," Tamara chimed in too loudly. "See where all those people are crowded? They're over there, and they're already sold out."

Her dad nodded thoughtfully and turned back to Will. "So how much do you think you'll pull in tonight?"

"I'll make a nice little profit. It's just something I do on the side."

It was too quiet, she panicked. Someone needed to say something. Now.

"Excuse me, Mr. Contreras, but Nadine asked me to get

Tamara for a second." Her dad speared Will with an un-
blinking stare.

"There's someone from *Los Angeles Magazine,* and they
want a photo of us." Will cleared his throat, shifted his
weight from one foot to the other. "It'll be just a second,
and I'll bring her right back."

Her dad smiled in that I'm-not-so-sure-about-you-yet
kind of way. "Go. And find out when the magazine comes
out, so I can buy a copy."

Tamara kissed his cheek. "I'll be right back."

"No you won't," he murmured. When the hell did
everyone get so damn emotional? "I like him."

Will took her arm, and together they walked across the
gallery. Inside she screamed, *You didn't come all the way up
here to fall in love! What the hell were you thinking?*

Will snuck his hand into hers and held on.

26

TAMARA WAS ABOUT to remind the caterers one last time that they needed to pull the back door shut to lock it properly when that familiar hand pressed into the small of her back.

"They'll figure it out." Will held her coat. "Let's go."

Tamara glanced across the gallery, meeting Nadine's ever-watchful eye as she sat on the edge of her desk while Holly added up the evening's sales.

She turned back to deliver a witty remark, but it evaporated when he moved, his breath heating her cheek. Her eyes drifted down to that serious mouth.

"I'm ready," she said.

Tamara walked with him outside, sucking in air that smelled sharply of wet pavement. God that felt good, she thought after spending five hours in a room that bulged with noise and body heat.

She looked up at the mist glittering under the beams of the streetlamps, then at him, admiring his stoic profile and the broad shoulders that looked strong enough to bear the burden of the world.

"I liked seeing your dad again," Will said, glancing down at her with a lopsided grin. "Your brother just stared at me like the last time."

"Sorry. But after he gets to know you it's impossible to shut him up."

He took her arm, guiding her around a pothole filled with oily water. "Where do you want to go?"

She wished he hadn't let go of her arm and pocketed his hand. "Home."

"Are you okay?"

She nodded.

"Sure?"

"What makes you think—"

"Excuse me," she thought she heard her mother say.

Recognition shot up Tamara's spine as she whirled around. Just to make sure her eyes worked right, Tamara said one word, "Mom?"

Susan stood just a few feet away, the wet wind playing with the end of an electric blue scarf tucked in the collar of her ankle-length brown coat. Susan stepped closer into the pool of pale light cast by a buzzing streetlamp.

"Hello, Tamara."

Tamara's heart clenched at the sound of hearing her mother speak her name. Her ears pounded, and a hot sheen of sweat broke out over her skin.

Her mother's lips trembled, and she unclasped her hands, then looked at Will. "Aren't you going to introduce me to your friend?"

Tamara couldn't have said her own name.

"Good evening, Mrs. Contreras." Will stepped forward, his hand held out. Tamara heard the whisper of his coat sleeve as he brushed past her. "I'm Will Benavides."

"Susanna Contreras," her mother said, using her full name, which only confirmed she hated him. He clasped her mother's fingers, then drew back beside Tamara.

"I'm not interrupting anything, am I?" her mom asked.

Tamara shook her head. Still too stunned by her appearance, by the fact that her mother was actually there, *talking* to her, she couldn't yet achieve brain-mouth coordination.

Susan retreated a step. "I didn't . . . maybe I should just go and come back another time."

"No." Tamara reached out like she would in a dream. But unlike a dream her hand caught and held on to her mother's arm. "We can go inside. I have a key."

Please don't leave. "Come inside and at least have a cup of tea," Tamara coaxed.

"Tamara, I'll see you tomorrow," Will said. She turned when he gave her arm a gentle squeeze. She hoped he saw the apology in her eyes. He grinned as if he understood.

"It was nice meeting you, Mrs. Contreras." He turned on his heel and left them.

She turned back to her mother, realizing her fingers dug into her coat sleeve. She released, then clasped her hands in front of her.

"Well . . ." She grasped for something to say. "Did it take you long to find us?"

"I got a little turned around when I got off the freeway," Susan said, falling into step beside Tamara. "Is this a very dangerous neighborhood?"

"We haven't had any problems. I mean, as long as you're aware of your surroundings and don't walk alone at night."

"Hmmm."

When they reached the gallery, they paused as the caterers carried the banquet table out the front door. Tamara smelled Nadine's and Jesse's cigarette smoke drifting down the hall.

She tried not to visibly cringe when she saw her mother sniffing the air.

"This is Will's work." Her voice boomed off the walls as she pointed to one of the canvases.

She noticed that her mother studied the painting longer than the other pieces in the collection.

Jesse's laugh, the kind that could break glass, drifted down the hallway.

"I should close the door," Tamara murmured.

She let herself breathe a moment.

Even though they had said terrible things to each other, they treated each other with this oddly polite, nervous civility.

This was her new life and her friends. But as much as she tried to train herself not to care what her mother thought, Tamara edged over to her desk, which had been returned to its rightful place, and found herself hoping that she approved.

"What are the red stickers for?" Susan asked, eyeing Tamara's suit. When she made no comment, Tamara almost heard another check next to her name in the bad-daughter column.

"That means the canvas is sold." Tamara straightened

off the desk, running her hand down her jacket. "All of Will's paintings sold tonight."

She cleared her throat, then brought her hands together. "So what exactly did you do?"

"I arranged for all the work to arrive at the gallery, and I put the reception together."

Her mother nodded as she strolled to a pile of catalogs. "Did you do anything for this?"

Tamara smiled and struggled to keep it. "I sent all the copy and photos to the designer."

"I don't see your name in it."

Tamara clenched her teeth, listening to the crinkle of pages as her mother flipped through it.

"So you moved all the way up here just for this?"

"I'm the gallery assistant. I'm going to be in two magazines next month."

Susan lifted an eyebrow, then shut the catalog.

"I have a lot of responsibility," Tamara insisted. "And this experience will help me with my applications to grad school."

"Well, I'm just surprised. I guess I thought because you went to such lengths to change your career plans that you would've . . . done more." She crossed her arms over her chest. "I can't imagine you make enough to pay for an apartment by yourself."

"I also work nights at the coffeehouse next door."

"Oh right." Her mother turned to look out the window, then back at Tamara. "Serving tables and making people coffee with a bachelor's degree and a teaching credential."

Tamara's inner Mama's girl told her to just take it; she'd never won when she took her mother on.

But the months away from her mother had created a stronger voice. One who wasn't going to take any shit on her turf.

"I've learned how to deal with artists, how to plan an installation, and how to talk with a patron. I pay for my own apartment and my own things."

She stopped herself just to before delivering a stinging, *I didn't need to get married like you did.*

Her mother straightened at the challenge. "Still, I can't imagine you're making what you made as a teacher."

"Money isn't everything," Tamara tossed back, crossing her arms.

Her mother laughed dryly. "It is when you want a future, sweetie."

"I'm applying for my master's degree."

"That costs even more money," she said. After a moment she lobbed another bomb, "What if you don't get in?"

"Then I'll figure it as—"

"I know this has been a big step for you, but I don't see where it's going to take you," her mother explained patiently. "Can't you teach part-time and go to school? What if there're no jobs after you get this master's degree?"

"Mom, stop." Tamara uncrossed her arms, determined to stand strong. "I'm proud of what I've done because it's the first thing I've earned on my own. And yes, my name is in the catalog on the back page of the acknowledgments section. Maybe I'm a glorified secretary, but here I'm not just your daughter or Ruben's girlfriend or some old homecoming queen. They want me here because I can do the job. Why can't you respect that? Why do you have to be like Grandma and make me feel like nothing?"

Trying not to wish she could take it back, Tamara looked away from her mother. Any second now she would hear her walk right back out of her life.

Her head jerked up when her mother moved. Right before her eyes, her mother's face crumpled. She pressed one hand to her forehead as a sob waved up and out of her.

"Mom?" Tamara stopped her hand just short of touching her mother's quaking shoulders.

There was a special place in Hell for daughters who made their mothers cry. They probably had a waiting list, but after all she pulled in the last six months, Tamara was headed straight to the front of the line.

She let her hand land on Susan's back, then warily stepped closer until she held her mother in a half hug. "Mom, don't cry. I didn't mean it. I was mad, and I shouldn't have said that."

Vaguely she heard the back door open and quickly shut.

"I came here after I realized that I've never missed any of your special things." Susan took in a deep breath before continuing. "I went to every piano recital, every game when you were a cheerleader, and all the open houses."

Tamara leaned her head on her mom's shoulder.

"Remember?" Susan asked.

Tamara began crying silently with her mom. There had never been an award or milestone without her.

"This is the first and the only one I missed," Susan said tightly.

She didn't see when her mom turned to fully embrace her. It just seemed to happen.

"I'm sorry, too," Tamara said. "For going behind your back like I did, and saying you're li—"

Her mom's hold tightened. She felt soft, strong, and delicate all at the same time. "Yes you should be, but I'm sorry for not being there for you.

"No matter how much I swore and promised, I still heard myself say the things my mother said or do the things she did." Susan shivered, and Tamara held on to her tighter. "I've said terrible things to you."

Tamara swallowed against her swelling throat. "I did, too."

Her mom's breath shuddered. "Do you know what really makes me proud of you? That you never called for help. You did this on your own.

"I'm proud that you did this," Susan said, her breath hitching. "I made my life the way I wanted it to be, and now you're making your own."

"But you don't approve."

"No I don't. But it's your life, and you need to live with the consequences, whatever they are."

"There goes my makeup," Tamara muttered as she looked down at her finger, smudged with black mascara.

Her mom gripped her by both arms. "I want you to remember this so you don't treat my grandchildren like this."

"Okay." Tamara's voice wobbled, but she managed to smile weakly. "But it might be a while before you get those grandchildren."

Her mother blinked, then sniffled. "What about the young man I met outside? He looks like a very nice boy."

Some things never changed. "Mom, don't get started."

"Well, he looks like he cares for you," she insisted as she pulled her purse around and started digging through it.

"And he's talented. His work is the best out of all these."
She pointed with a travel-sized bag of Kleenex.

Tamara knew what her mom was thinking—*the two of them will give me such artistic grandbabies*—and she didn't want to like that idea.

"Will and I still have things to work out, and it's a little . . ." She struggled for the right word. "Premature."

"Premature?" Susan rolled her eyes. "Your generation makes things too complicated."

"Mom." Tamara blew her nose. "I'm still working towards getting my degree and after that I don't know where I'll have to move to get a job. There's no room for a wedding or a baby between now and then."

"So this means you're not coming home before you'll start school?"

Tamara shook her head, deciding that San Francisco was too much for both of them to handle right now. "I think I'll be staying in L.A."

"So Will lives here in L.A., no?" her mother asked.

"Yes, but don't get any ideas. I'm not getting married for at least another three or four years."

The pursed lips and the knowing stare said, *Not if I have anything to do with it.*

But at least she kept it to herself. And for her mother, that was a start.

27

WILL STILL HADN'T DECIDED if he did the right thing when he shut his truck door and walked to the back gate. Should he have waited in the parking lot? But if he'd waited, he wouldn't have given Tamara and her mother the privacy they needed.

And what would her mother have thought if they walked out to find him sitting in the dark like some stalker?

Then again, that part of downtown crawled with transients, drug dealers, and God only knew what. Even though the café would still be open and the caterers had still been cleaning up when he left, the parking lot was a vast wasteland of darkness.

He was about to undo the latch when the gate edged open. Adrenaline powered through his blood as he stood back ready to deck the person on the other side.

An old man in a suit halted in surprise, his hand poised with a fedora over his head.

"What are you doing here?" Will demanded, falling back into command voice from his days in the Corps.

"*Con permiso* . . . I . . . ahh." The man chuckled warily, then remembered to put his hat on his head. "*Con permiso.*"

Will relaxed enough to take a good look at the old, but well-made double-breasted suit and the polished oxfords.

"I'm Julius Aguilar," the man said, holding out his hand.

Will shook it. The old man had strength. He admired that. "Will Benavides. I live above the garage."

Julius grinned, the corners of his lips twitching from the effort. "I know all about you. Mati—" He cleared his throat. "Doña Allende speaks very highly of you."

Will had to give it to him, Julius Aguilar was pretty suave about leaving a seventy-six-year-old woman's house at midnight.

He swallowed the urge to grin. "May I ask you a question, sir?"

"*Ah. Sí. Por favor.*"

Will crossed his arms, widening his stance. "Are you and Señora Allende uh . . . special friends?"

Julius's lips tightened. "I don't see how that is your business."

"It's my business if you hurt her." Señora Allende would've gasped, then slapped him if she overheard this. "You know, it's okay if you leave out the front door."

"Ma—" Julius quickly corrected himself. "Doña Allende is very discreet."

Will looked down at the ground, hiding a grin. Sneaky would be more like it.

He wondered if he and Tamara would still have that spark when they were Julius's and Señora Allende's ages.

If, he corrected, they could just get on with it while they were still in their twenties.

He backed down. "Sorry," he said. "I didn't mean to be rude."

Still bristling, Julius nodded as he walked past Will. He stopped abruptly, then ground his heel against the sidewalk.

Will turned in case the old man was going to deck him. *"Esta la luz de mi vida,"* Julius said.

"Good." Will stopped himself from asking what he was going to do about her moving away.

Julius grinned as he tipped his hat. "I hope she'll get around to introducing us. Till then, this will be our *secreto.*" He headed across the street, past the church toward his house, the only one with the porch light on.

Will pocketed one hand, then went into the backyard, securing the bolt before following the path to his apartment. He wished Tamara was with him. The uneasy question came back with a bite as he thought what he was willing to do to keep her here with him.

The choice was hers. He knew how much she wanted her gallery and dammit, maybe if he was more of an asshole, he wouldn't care if her staying with him meant that she'd lose that dream.

But he loved her enough that he would let her go if that's what she wanted.

Tamara pulled behind Will's truck, then killed the engine. Still holding on to the wheel, she slumped in her seat. Although her body felt heavy and her eyes sandy, her brain hummed. She hoped Will was still awake. She couldn't wait until morning to tell him about her mom and just be with him.

Maybe she should've called him instead. Out of respect for Señora Allende, they stayed at Tamara's place when she was home. This time she wouldn't spend the night. They'd talk, then she'd go home. Or he'd go with her.

Her fingers danced on the steering wheel. This was getting way out of control. Nadine was right, the sex thing between them glared like neon. But then there were times when they just palled around, doing nothing more complicated than holding hands or sitting across from each other at a meal.

She leaned forward to start the engine, then saw his silhouette walk in front of the windows above the garage. A little smile touched her lips.

Tamara heaved the door open, taking a moment to watch the rain clouds sweep across the sky. She made her way into the backyard and climbed up to the top of his stairs.

He must have heard her coming because the doorknob turned, and he stood right there, in a thin white T-shirt and sweatpants.

"I didn't wake you up, did I?" she asked softly.

"I was hoping you'd stop by," he said.

She walked into his tiny kitchen.

"How did it go with your mom?" He shut the door and flipped the lock.

"Good. It was rough at first, but she and I . . . we're kinda back to normal." She paused as he leaned forward for a kiss, a simple uncomplicated kiss.

Their lips clicked when he pulled away. He didn't do

anything more. No hands around the waist, no whispered promises in her ear.

She followed him into his living room. "My mom really liked your work. And she wants me to bring you to dinner."

"Yeah? And what did you say?"

"I told her I'd think about it," she said playfully.

"Think about what?"

Did he somehow sense that she was having second thoughts? Not that she was. Well, sort of. Oh God, she remembered. Did he overhear her conversation with Nadine?

All of her thoughts ground to a halt when Tamara glimpsed the painting propped up against the wall.

His work always stopped her short. The intensity of color, the eerily realistic treatment, and the almost naked emotion he froze in paint. Sometimes she wondered if he'd sold his soul to the Devil for his talent. But this . . .

"This is the canvas you showed me that day," she said, drawn to stand up close. "When Nadine sees this, she'll go nuts."

"I'm not selling it."

Tamara leaned closer, seeing something familiar about the little boy clutching a stick in his hand. Her eyes studied the older boy standing with the woman, who was twisted away in a weird position on the bench.

"Who are they?" she asked, feeling him standing beside her.

Will didn't answer right away. "That's my mother, my brother Ricky, and me."

Awareness needled through her. She held her breath as

it dawned on her that he might finally unlock the door that she could never open inside of him.

"I didn't know you had a brother." She turned when he stayed clammed up. "What happened to him?"

His eyes stayed fixed on the canvas, still holding on to that part of himself he kept from her.

"He was shot at a football game when I was twelve."

"Oh, Will—"

He shifted his weight to his other leg, putting just a little more distance between them. The refrigerator hummed from its dark corner.

Tamara studied the older boy in the painting closer. Will painted his face in profile, but she could see the concern in the boy's eyes, in the way he reached out to his mother on the bench.

"He always encouraged me to draw and stuff. He caught me when I was six, and at first I thought he'd beat me up, because he was always trying to toughen me up. But when I got tired of jumping up and down to get my drawing back, he told me they were good."

A sad grin touched his lips. Tamara stood absolutely still, afraid of shattering the spell.

"He . . . we were always getting kicked out of our apartments. So after that Ricky was always signing me up for these contests at the library and you know, I can still remember the first one I won."

"Do you remember what you drew?"

His eyes flicked to her, looking for something. Right in the center of her chest, she hurt for the little boy who only had his brother to realize he'd been special.

"Batman. Ricky even went with me to turn it in. After

we left he went on and on about how I was going to win. I told myself it was just some stupid library contest and by the time they got around to picking the winners, we'd probably have to move anyway.

"But um . . . I won. I got second place."

"No one knows genius when they see it," she whispered, getting a little smile out of him.

He lifted one shoulder, then shifted his weight from one foot to the other. His eyes went back to the painting. "So anyway, there was this one morning when we woke up and she"—he pointed to his mother—"had breakfast ready. We were lucky if we got cereal. Anyway, she told us we were going to take the bus to a job interview. But she took us to social services."

Her throat squeezed tight as she realized that gifted little boy in the painting had no idea he'd have to face the world without the brother who shouldered a sagging backpack.

"Will, I—"

"Don't." He saw the pity swimming in her eyes. Her pity was the last thing he wanted.

She blinked, then pressed her lips together. "What happened after she took you to social services?"

"What do you think?"

"I don't know, Will," she said evenly.

He grinned against the hollowness that yawned in his chest. "You don't want to hear about my shit, Tamara."

"Yes I do." Her eyes dropped down as he moved in closer. "You know all about mine. But I've been waiting for you to tell me yours."

"Oh, so am I that easy to read?"

"Please don't. Talk to me. Finish what you started."

"You feel sorry for me, don't you?"

When she didn't answer, he folded his arms across his chest. "My mother was released from prison four years ago and is living in fucking Mexico. My dad is doing life at San Quentin for holding down a nineteen-year-old girl while his buddy stabbed her to death."

Her eyes widened to the size of plates. "We had different lives, Tamara. You can't understand. I can see that on your face."

He knocked her back with the anger he aimed at her. The last thing he expected was for her to come back swinging.

"She dropped you off at social services, then what? Did they separate you from Ricky? Put you in different foster homes and maybe let you guys visit each other every now and then."

She'd read his life just like that, then matched his stance by crossing her arms, meeting him eye to eye. "I was a teacher for one year and worked in classrooms as an assistant for two years before that. I worked with kids who were in foster homes. I even took a class on how to deal with troubled children. Maybe I grew up with two parents, a brother, and a dog, but I'm not the naive moron everyone thinks I am."

When he said nothing she turned on her heel and reached for her coat. "I wasted ten years with a guy who patronized and constantly second-guessed me. I won't do that ever again."

It was best to let her leave. She'd walk sooner or later.

She had plans that didn't include him. Hell, he'd even helped her send those applications off.

But the pain of watching her shove her arms in the coat with her back turned to him was the worst pain he'd ever felt. Worse than the moment when the social worker, with the little apple-shaped buttons on her blouse, dragged him away from his crying brother.

"Come here." In two strides he had her pulled against him. His mouth took hers in one of those ruthless, lust-ridden kisses that left no questions about what he wanted.

28

"I KNOW WHAT you're trying to do," Tamara whispered when he kissed that place next to her ear that he knew weakened her knees.

His hands impatiently tugged her blouse out of her pants. "Why are you wearing this thing?"

She gasped when he grabbed her hips and ground her against him so she could feel him against her thigh.

With equal force, Tamara tugged his face up and pulled away so he had to hold her from falling back. "Stop it."

Will yanked her forward, then released her as her pity burned him. She wouldn't see the raw pain from the scar he just peeled back for her to see.

"They separated you, didn't they?"

With no other options, he nodded.

"Where did they take you? Your grandmother?"

"Yeah."

"Did his foster family hurt him?"

"Probably."

She softened her stance and he looked away.

"Why did he die?"

"He was in a gang. His family lived in Boyle Heights. He started dealing drugs and owed some other guy money. So they found him at a football game and shot him in the parking lot."

He heard her feet move over the carpet and felt her take him in her arms. "I was with my friends watching the game."

She said nothing, asked no questions. Her arms were so much smaller than his that she could barely touch her fingertips together across his back. But she clung to him like she'd never let go.

They stood that way while the clock in his bedroom ticked off the seconds. Tears squeezed out the corners of his eyes, and his whole body trembled as the old hurt wafted up and out of him. And she held him through the pain until it slowly ebbed away in the way a storm relinquished the ocean until it quietly lapped against the sand.

Tamara felt the tension in him slacken and gently ran her hand up then down his spine. "Can I stay with you tonight?" she whispered.

He nodded, then pulled away from her, holding himself in a way to hide the tears she'd felt through her hair. Will made a straight line for the lights. There was nothing left to say after this battle.

She wasn't even sure who won as she pulled off her coat and followed him into his bedroom.

They crawled into bed, her in her underwear; him in his sweats and shirt. Side by side, face-to-face, they fell asleep.

Tamara slept so hard that she only remembered part of a dream. One of those dreams where she was doing one thing, then suddenly she was in some other city that was San Francisco but wasn't.

She and Will were walking through Olvera Street, trying to hold hands in a stew of people who wouldn't step out of their way. And then their grip broke apart, but she sensed him behind her, keeping up as she walked sideways through the crowd. Eventually she broke clear and stood in Will's bedroom with Nadine and Isa asking her where she wanted her dishes. But Will's bedroom was in San Francisco, and she was crying because he was gone.

Tamara woke up, feeling him run his finger over her cheek and hearing the sound of rain pattering on the roof. Her eyes flipped open, and they stared at one another. He didn't smile, didn't speak. He scooted closer, and their lips met again.

She hooked her arm over his shoulder and nudged closer, intertwining her leg between his. Not caring if she hadn't brushed her teeth or washed away the sweat from running nonstop at the gallery the night before, she kissed him.

He left her lips wet. "Tell me this is what you want," he whispered.

His muscles bunched under the feather-light brush of her hand. "Say it, Tamara," he urged.

"Yes, I want you."

Holding her gaze prisoner with his, his warm hand traveled up from her waist to skim his knuckles just over the top of her bra.

Burning to feel her naked against him, Will rolled onto his back, pulled off his sweats and shirt.

He had slept in fits, some part of him fearing that she'd

leave. And when his eyes opened to find her still sleeping
beside him, he listened to her breathing, knowing he loved
her.

Without any warning she appeared above him. Her liq-
uid eyes told him she was in control as she slipped her bra
off so he could see her pointed nipples in the gray light of
the morning.

She leaned forward, and their lips played again while
their hands traveled over each other.

He could give her more time to fall in love with him.
She wouldn't be here if she felt nothing. He knew that
much about her heart.

"Tamara," he begged, when her fingers wound around
him. He always pleasured her first, always made love to
her. But her hand tightened with each groan he made, and
the wet kisses she planted on his chest would've made a
lesser man lose it.

Those sensations were nothing compared to the wet
heat of her tongue.

Will didn't care if Tamara's name could be heard up and
down the block. His whole world was the light stretched
out over the ceiling and what she was doing to him with
her mouth.

He shivered when her mouth left him, then looked
down. If he died right now, he'd take the sight of her with
the light awakening the room as she loomed over him.
Tamara in real life, in his bed, was better than any fantasy
he'd had in the past.

"You didn't have to do that," he said, even as his hips
arched up for mercy.

"I know. Even though I want you inside me, and I get

turned on just thinking about us together, this isn't the only thing that I want from you, Will."

She sat on the tops of his thighs, sliding her wet hand over him. "Don't ever think that all I want is to fuck you."

He sprang up, catching her by the arms and rolling on top of her. One hand went to the wet V of her thighs and the other to her breast. Like an animal, his teeth scraped hers. She moaned into his mouth as his thumb wound lazy circles, and his fingers sank into her.

"I need you now," he growled as he reared his hips, then slid right into her.

She cried his name, nearly bucking him off her.

He planted his hands on either side of her head and bent to kiss her tenderly. He tortured them both with long, slow strokes.

The wet sound of their joining and her insistent grip on him drove him faster and harder. Their mouths met as they tried to reach that scalding moment that promised nothing yet everything. It took her over first as she twisted her mouth free, and she tightened all around him like a vise.

And then he was free. Something escaped from the deepest chamber of his heart, throwing him under a twisting, somersaulting wave that threatened to drown him.

As their breathing settled, they gripped hands. Her head turned, bumping lightly against his.

He nuzzled her neck, never wanting to spend another night without her. He wanted to wake up every morning so he could hold her just like this, her pulse beating in his ear and her softness against him.

She kissed his neck where the pulse beat. Will shut his

eyelids, hoping to squeeze out the tears that came from nowhere.

With nothing left—no pride, no secrets—he whispered, "I love you."

Her legs loosened their hold around his waist. And he felt her chest depress as the breath released itself. He lifted himself up so he could look down at her.

She smiled. "I love you, too, Will."

29

April of this year

TAMARA PRESSED HER HAND against the glass, watching her mother kneeling over her baby plants. A grin eased over her lips as she heard her mom talking to them. In her hand she held the letter from USC she'd pulled out of her mailbox just an hour ago. It was suspiciously slimmer than the acceptance package she received from San Francisco State.

Even a few days shy of twenty-seven years old, and there were times like this when a girl still needed her mother.

So Tamara came home on a Thursday afternoon when she knew her mom would be on spring break, working on her garden.

"Did you pick up the things I asked for?" her mom asked, when Tamara pushed the sliding glass door open.

"Sorry, wrong child."

Tamara heard the snap in her mom's back when she

snapped up like a spring. "M'ija? What did you do to your hair?"

Tamara silenced her with a fierce abrazo. "Like it?"

Her mom's eyes fastened on the sleek Louise Brooks bob. "But it was so nice long. What does Will think of this?"

Some things would never change, and for once Tamara didn't mind.

"I'm sure he's planning to leave me any day," she answered dryly.

Muttering something about mouthy kids, Susan pushed herself up using the ledge of the vegetable box Memo and Ruben had built for her two summers ago. "Are you hungry? You drove all the way down here, so you're staying for dinner. And where's Will?"

"He's on duty."

Tamara caught the quick glance at her middle. "Is everything okay?" She slapped her soiled gloves against her muddy jeans.

"Why don't we open this and find out?" She held up the envelope.

"Oh Díos." Susan's hand flew up to her neck. "I need to sit down."

They each dusted off mismatched chairs around a table barely standing under her mom's binge at Home Depot.

"Where are you going to put all these plants, Mom?"

"The boys are building me another planter back there." She took a deep breath. "Well? Open the letter."

Tamara shoved her thumb beneath the flap, wincing when the paper sliced into the web of skin. She peeked and saw a single trifolded letter. She knew.

Disgusted, she slapped it on the table.

"What?" Susan asked, both hands gripping the arms of her chair. "Is it bad?"

"I didn't get in."

"You didn't read it." She snatched up the envelope and pulled out the letter.

"The rejection letter I got last year looked the same," Tamara explained, as her mom unfolded and read it. Unlike the first time, she felt nothing but white noise screaming through her. No loss, not even panic. Just numb.

"Tamara!" Her mom's nails dug into her knee. "You're number two on the wait list!" She waved the letter like a madwoman. "¡Mira!"

Grasping it with both hands, Tamara's eyes raced over the praise of her accomplishments, her risk-taking spirit, and the difficult decision in which they selected among the highly qualified pool of candidates. But the cold bare fact remained: She was two short of making the cut.

"Shit!"

Primly Susan scolded, "Watch your language." And in the same breath, "M'ija, you still have a chance on the wait list."

"They accepted three," Tamara answered, feeling the bitterness burn the back of her throat. "So if even one drops, I still won't get in."

"But what if the person ahead of you decides to go somewhere else?"

Tamara crumpled the letter in her fist.

Her mom sighed and took her hand, uncurling her fingers. "You could keep working at the gallery and try again next year."

Tamara stared ahead and saw so many uncertainties. USC could call her next week or never. Or she could go to San Francisco. "If I do that, I'll be another year behind."

"Tamara, you're only twenty-six years old."

"When you were my age, you were already a teacher and you had me, then two years later you had Memo. You were set. I'm starting all over again."

"Not really." Susan straightened the letter, sitting back in her chair thoughtfully. "I always wanted my own restaurant."

"You did?"

She nodded. "But with your grandmother it was out of the question, then I met your father, and we eloped—"

"Wait a second. You never told me you eloped."

"Honey, do the math. I was expecting you, and my mother, God rest her soul, would've killed us both."

Tamara couldn't quite picture her parents young and sneaking around so they had to get married.

"M'ija, how many times have you looked at our wedding picture?"

"I thought you were on a budget."

Her mom straightened. "We were."

"So why did you end up teaching if it wasn't what you wanted?"

"We needed the money, and it was something I was good at."

This couldn't be right. If Tamara knew one thing about her mom, it was that she didn't just grasp at what life randomly offered. She pushed, bullied, and plotted her way through it. For God's sake, the woman organized her outfits on the left side of her closet by the day of the week.

"Do you regret you didn't get your restaurant?"

"Not anymore." Her mom tucked the refolded letter in the envelope like she'd said nothing out of the ordinary. "So how long do you have until you need to confirm your acceptance at San Francisco State?"

"Another month." The woman sitting on the other side of the table looked like her mother, sounded like her, too. Except when Tamara looked at her now, she saw someone completely different than who she thought she was. "But don't you wonder what your life would've been like if you had?"

"Had what?"

"Decided differently. Not met Dad, rebelled against Grandma. What if you could've had what you wanted?"

Her mom inhaled deeply as she caressed the leaf of a tender basil plant. "I used to. And then it wasn't important anymore. I had two kids, a husband, and a career I loved. What I wanted as a girl didn't matter anymore."

"Do you think I should go to San Francisco?"

"As your mother, no," she admitted. "But that's not my decision."

Scooting to the edge of her chair, Tamara said, "But if you were in my place, would you go?"

Her mom looked at her for what felt like forever. "If you love Will, and he loves you like I know he does, then you'll figure it out."

Tamara sighed at the irony of it all. The one time she came to her mother needing to be told what to do, the woman got all philosophical and hands-offish.

"M'ija, I know it sounds simple, but you just never know where life takes you." She slid the envelope to

Tamara's side of the table. "And no matter how hard you plan and try, you just have to decide with your heart."

"You've just made my decision that much harder. Thanks."

Her mom smiled softly. "I really like Will."

"You liked Ruben, too."

"Ruben was a good man but not good for you. But Will, he's good for you."

Tamara always loved her mother, but now she was starting to like her, too.

"So does this mean that you . . . I mean even though I didn't get in that you're—" Tamara decided she didn't want to go there.

"What, m'ija?"

"Nothing."

They sat quietly. The Glenmens next door had Oprah turned up loud enough for them to hear the audience cheering.

"I am," her mom said.

"You're what?"

"Proud of you. That's what you were asking me, right?"

"Yeah."

"I'm glad you shared it with me first."

Tamara smiled even though the burden of her decision remained on her shoulders. "Me too."

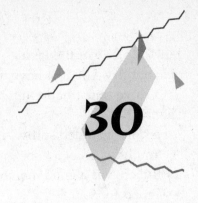

That Saturday

TAMARA WAS GOING to tell Will.

Really.

Just not now. Or even after Señora Allende's party. Maybe tomorrow, in the evening. Late tomorrow evening. Tamara drew in her breath, sitting in her car with Will's going-away gift wedged behind the seats. She stared at the minivan that had run out of room for any more MY CHILD IS A GOOD CITIZEN AT JFK ELEMENTARY bumper stickers.

That could be her if she played it safe and stayed here with him.

Or, maybe not. Maybe there was a chance two people would drop from USC, and she and the other guy ahead of her could get in.

It could happen.

What a nightmare. She'd met Señora Allende's three daughters last night when she came over to help Will move tables. After five minutes with them she'd swore the oldest one, Anita, looked straight into her uterus, and asked, "No baby yet?"

Tamara drummed the tips of her nails on the steering wheel. She wanted to stay with Will in this city that she'd also fallen in love with. That was a given. But could she stay if that meant giving up possibly the only sure shot she had been given?

The last damn thing she wanted right now was to attend a party. Especially with Señora Allende's evil daughters lingering around with their questions and knowing looks. But Will needed her. He didn't have to say it. His longer silences, the more time he spent in his studio, said it for him.

With a deep breath, she got out of the car, determined to be the perfect albeit baby-free cohostess of Señora Allende's farewell party. But first, she'd figure out how to free the canvas from her backseat.

"Hey, babe, let me help you with that," Will called from the front door. Seeing him jog down the short path to the front gate made her heart trip and her senses grow keener with the awareness of him.

"How is it in there?" she asked. Will slid his hand behind her head and kissed her. She kept her eyes open; with his closed, Will appeared vulnerable.

Knowing that Señora Allende's daughters were probably spying on them, Tamara placed her hands on his shoulders and gently pushed him back.

"Let's not give them a free show." She drew her hands down his arms. "So?"

His mouth thinned with tension. "She's up to something." He wiped her lipstick off his mouth with the back of his hand. "Did I get it all off?"

"Yep."

"Let me carry this inside."

She stepped aside so he could bend down into the car to pull out the canvas she picked up from the framers at the last minute.

This felt right, standing here with him, doing things for him. They'd gotten to the point where he didn't flinch when she bought a box of tampons in front of him.

"Are you coming in?"

"What?"

He held the canvas against his chest. "Are you okay?"

"Wha—" She shook her head, eager to get inside and away from this hamster-in-a-wheel thing in her head. "Yeah. Fine."

"Sure about that?"

He made a move like he was going to kiss her, and she slammed the car door shut. "Yep. Great. Let's go."

She wasn't proud of it. But she knew she was running as fast as she could.

When the husbands—or the "outlaws" as Señora Allende called them—filed out of the TV room, Will knew whatever boiled under the surface of the evening was about to explode. He tipped back his bottle of beer, catching Señor Aguilar jovially leering at Señora Allende.

"The youngest one, Sarah, now she looks like Matilda," he said. He tipped his Cuban-style fedora when Señora Allende looked their way. "*Que bella.* Not too many like her around, eh?"

Will wasn't sure he wanted to hear any of this.

"So what are you going to do about your Tamara? She's a beauty too, eh?"

"What are you going to do about Señora Allende leaving?" Will asked dryly.

Señor Aguilar looked at him in surprise, then laughed, patting Will on the back. "It's not what I'm going to do, it's what I did, m'ijo."

Ignoring the fact that the old man called him "m'ijo," Will watched Tamara emerge from the kitchen, led by the hand of one of Señora Allende's grandsons.

She was holding back on him. She'd been tossing and turning beside him at night for a week. But he didn't pry, didn't push . . . didn't try to talk her into any decisions. Even the one he wanted her to make.

Now as he watched one woman walk out of his life, he wasn't sure how he could let Tamara do the same.

"Don't think too hard about it," Señor Aguilar teased; apparently he could also read minds. "Because when you're thinking, that's when they get away."

Holding on to *this much* of his last nerve, Will was about to let the old man have it. But Señor Aguilar handed him his beer and walked toward Señora Allende who stood in the center of the party.

"Peter, cut the music," she demanded.

The music cut off.

"Julius, *venga aca!*"

Tamara watched Will from where she stood on the steps, crossing her arms against the late-afternoon chill. She smiled faintly.

"Mama," Anita drawled, when Señor Aguilar took her

mother's hand, kissed it, then rested his other hand on top of it. "What's going on?"

Ignoring her, Señora Allende stood shoulder to shoulder with him. "First, I want to thank all of you for my twenty-sixth birthday party," she said.

The old ladies laughed in a girlish chorus. Her eldest daughter, Anita, lifted her chin, then planted fists on hips, while her sisters exchanged clueless glances.

"But truly, the year leading up to this moment has been a difficult one. One that I had no idea would force me to look at my life and realize that the chapter as an independent woman has come to an end."

As she spoke, Will's mind cataloged the memories of coming home to Señora Allende. Some mornings she would have him sit with her over sweet rolls and café con leche. Or she would finagle him into moving her furniture while she spring-cleaned.

Those little things accumulated into a relentless riptide of memories that pulled him close to the depth of his love for her.

"I will miss all of my very good friends who have grown up with me as young wives, mothers, and now grandmothers. Many of us are coming up on those years when we must decide if we can continue to live alone or con sus familías. I have chosen to do both."

Señora Allende and Señor Aguilar looked at each other with expressions so plain with love, that Will wondered if he'd been wrong about the old bastard.

"Julius asked me to marry him, and I not only said yes, but I went ahead and married him yesterday."

A plane droned overhead. The freeway hummed in the

distance. Tension charged through the air and rolled off skin like electricity.

"Mom?" Anita squeaked. "Wha—Where?"

"In a little chapel downtown."

"Downtown? Not even in a church?"

Señora Allende turned a regal frown on her daughter. "Why? You didn't."

Questions exploded all at once.

"Wait, wait!" Señora Allende pulled her other hand free, holding them both up for silence. "Now before everyone gets excited I need to make my second announcement."

She glanced over the crowd, stopping when she found Will. "M'ijo, I have a gift for you. Come."

Will felt the heat of dozens of eyes on him as he stepped into the circle with Señora Allende and Señor Aguilar, who handed her an envelope. She passed it to Will. "Open it," she encouraged.

Helpless, he glanced at Tamara. She looked just as bewildered but a helluva lot more amused than he felt about the whole thing.

He ripped it open and pulled out a folded paper. He read it twice . . . then a third time. His throat clenched like a fist. Through the noise in his head he heard Señora Allende announce, "It's the deed to my home."

She rested her trembling hand on his shoulder. "Will is the son I never had, and this has become—"

Her voice broke and her hand tightened its grip on his shirt. He heard someone, probably one of her comadres, sniffle.

"I don't want my home to go to strangers," Señora Allende continued, her voice rough with defiant emotion. *"Yo quiero que se quede en la familía."*

His breath hitched and before anyone saw the tears, he pulled her into an embrace. As they held each other, she whispered, "And don't waste any more time with Tamara. *¿Entiendes?"*

Loss clenched him by the throat.

"Listen to me. *El Camarón que se duerma, se lo lleve la corriente."*

He couldn't help but grin. *The shrimp that falls asleep is carried away by the current.* He'd only heard that one a million times. "It's not that easy."

"That's what we all think, even, when you're old like mi esposo over there. But when it comes to love, you don't wait around." She dug her nails into his arm to make him realize she meant business. "Now go get your novia, m'ijo, before mis hijas get a hold of you."

31

"**W**HAT TIME DO YOU want to go?"

Tamara dropped the glass back into the sink. Soapy water spit up on the front of her shirt.

Will looked at her with that suspicious look of his. Good thing they were alone after Señora Allende had gathered her comadres in the sala with Will's painting of Señor Aguilar walking down a dark street propped up under her Virgin Mary altar.

After her announcement, Señora Allende's daughters whipped up their children and husbands, huffing out the whole way about how Señor Aguilar married their mother for her money, and it would never last.

Laughter exploded out of the sala.

"What's wrong with you?" Will asked, drying the plate he held in his hand.

"Nothing. I'm fine."

He put the plate down, tossed his dish towel on the counter, and came to stand right next to her. "No really. You've been different lately."

"There's a lot on my mind."

"I know. So what about my original question?"

"As soon as we're done here, but don't you want—"

He gripped her by both arms and kissed her.

"Will, they're just in the other room."

"You're not telling me something."

His question made her knees go weak.

"Tamara, I promised myself I wouldn't try to influence your decision. But I want to know—"

It was painful to look him in the eye.

"I feel like I'm losing everything that matters to me right now." His voice was rough with barely controlled emotion. "And I feel like I'm losing you."

"You're not going to lose me or even Señora Allende," she said softly.

"What does that mean?"

She edged away from him, needing just a second to think.

"Should I just take it that you don't want to hurt my feelings?" The silence yawned between them.

Her stomach melted away down her knees.

"I know how important your independence is to you and that you don't have everything figured out just yet, but this shouldn't be that hard," he said. "It wasn't that hard for me."

She opened her mouth to tell him, but something else came out instead. "I love you very much. But I just don't know what I'm going to do."

He stared at her like she'd just told him he had two months to live.

"I'm on the wait list for USC. Number two to be exact.

And you know about San Francisco already so . . . that's what I don't know."

"Think about this." His big hands that never seemed to get cold gently pried hers apart and held them. "I've loved you since we first met and believe me, if you want to go to San Francisco—"

She looked up when his voice broke, seeing his heart in those eyes.

"I can look into a lateral transfer to one of the departments up there. If you want me to."

"What about the house and your painting?"

"We'll rent the house, and I can paint anywhere. But I can't find another one like you." He squeezed her hand, letting her take it all in. "Whether we move up to San Francisco or stay here, none of that matters as long as we stay together."

Tamara decided right then and there. All her life she waited for someone, mainly her mother, to tell her what to do with her life. And this was no different except it was a one-hundred-year-old institution holding a decision over her head. This was what she wanted.

"I want to go to USC, and I want to stay here in L.A. And I want live together in this house with you."

His face that had once been such a mystery to her eloquently conveyed his surprise. "Are you sure?"

"I'm willing to take a chance." There, she said it. And lightning didn't strike. Feminists didn't storm the house.

She just wrapped her arms around him, and the back of her neck tingled as she held on.

Maybe one day she'd look back and see that San Francisco had been her only opportunity for another life. But she might not regret it.

Maybe. But what if she made the other choice and had to ache with regret over losing him?

Will pulled away to look back into her eyes.

"You're the only thing I've ever wanted," he said. "And the one person I thought I'd never have. I'll love you for the rest of your life."

He kissed her again with the night and with all the uncertainties surrounding them in the little house.

Tamara pulled back. "You'd better love me because you're going home with me to tell my mother."

Want More?

Turn the page to enter
Avon's Little Black Book—

the dish, the scoop and the
cherry on top from
MARY CASTILLO

Dime con quién andas
y te diré quién eres

(Tell me who you walk with, I'll tell you who you are)

The basics . . .

Full name: Mary Castillo

Why didn't you take your husband's name? Because I
didn't have to and he's confident in his masculinity.

Birthday? January 4.

Dogs or cats? Two pugs, Françoise and Rascal.

Profession? I've always made my living as a writer, having
done ad copy, PR, and reporting.

From the book . . .

Did you live in L.A.? Yes, for seven years, most of which
was spent in traffic on the 110.

Can you speak Spanish? Hahahahaha! Oh sorry. No.

**Will you ever admit which of your old bosses inspired Na-
dine?** I'm shocked you would ask that question! Nadine was
one of those characters who appeared fully formed and took
me along for the ride. So while I've had my share of *interesting* bosses, I can't say that I've had one quite like Nadine.

**What was the worst bridesmaid dress you ever had to
wear?** I've been lucky and wore two very cool bridesmaid's dresses. And I was a great bride I have to say. I let
my maid of honor choose her own dress. However, when
she asked if she could get a tattoo, I told her fine as long as
she understood my mom would be at my wedding.

**Did your parents support your decision to go to
USC?** At first no. It was too expensive, it was in the worst

part of L.A., and my dad had always been a Bruins fan. Also, the L.A. Riots of 1992 didn't help. But then I won a $10,000 scholarship three days before graduation, and my parents saw the value of telling all their friends, "My daughter is going to USC. You know, the University of Spoiled Children?" I graduated in 1996 with a degree in history and minor in cinema-television studies.

How long did you live at home with mom and dad? Eighteen years and the summer break after my freshman year. My parents' mantra to my brother and me was: "When you're eighteen you're out!" I listened, but it didn't take with my brother, who lives in a studio in front of their house.

How did your husband propose, and what did you say? He proposed New Year's Eve of 2000. We were squished into a corner table but he pulled out the little blue box with the white ribbon and I honestly thought they were earrings I'd pointed out before Christmas. After I flipped open the lid and stared at my ring, he got down on one knee, and asked me, "Mary, would you do me the honor of being my wife?" It took me a moment because everyone in the room whispered, "They're getting married!"

Then Ryan widened his eyes as if to say, come on, and I remembered that it was my turn to say yes. The restaurant burst into applause, and an older gentleman with a paper crown on his head asked if Ryan got a yes. When my husband told the room that I'd agreed, the old guy replied, "You better. That ring's from Tiffany's!"

What is the craziest thing you've ever done on a date? I once got into a pillow fight with my date in a very chichi furniture story in Santa Monica. I married him five years later.

How did you know he was the one? On our first Halloween together, he got our cat a pumpkin. The cat later ran away.

Is there anyone in your past that you ever think of as the one that got away? My husband will be reading this, you know. Let's just say that if I hadn't married him, he would've been the one who got away.

Where did you find Mrs. Allende's sayings? I found a book in a dusty Monterey store called *Old Spanish Sayings*. And there's a Mexican restaurant down the street that gives out fortune cookies called dichos. I found, *"El bien no es conocido hasta que es perdido"* (Good things are not appreciated until they are lost) from one of those.

Finally, what's up with the Wonder Woman references? In preschool my goal was to be Wonder Woman. My Grandma Nana made me a very authentic costume with little white stars sewn onto the pants with a cape, crown, bracelets, yellow yarn lasso, and knee-high boots dyed red. I trained every day in that costume and boots until the big Tiny Tots Halloween party. I then tied Frankenstein to a tree and my mom had to be called to release him. The costume is framed in my office.

On writing . . .

Who gave you the idea to become an author? My Grandma Margie once remarked to me that the best job in the world had to be an author. You can live anywhere you want, work when you want, and make up stories. Sounded pretty good to me.

What items are on your desk? A laptop, Wonder Woman blotter, can of pens and pencils, thesaurus, dictionary, The Observation Deck (a deck of cards with writing prompts), *How to Make Friends in Mexico* (a Spanish-English phrase book), and Schott's *Original Book of Miscellany*.

Favorite piece of wisdom on writing? Nora Roberts always says, "You can't fix a blank page." She's right.

Do you have a ritual before you get started writing every day? Since I'm still working full-time, I don't have time for rituals except on the weekends. I write during my lunch hour and two hours after dinner each night. On weekends, I walk in with a cup of tea and a glass of water, put on some music and maybe light a candle and give thanks for the privilege of getting paid to write. The pugs wrestle around before they settle into their bed by the window. Once they start snoring, I start writing. My goal has always been five pages a day, but I average between ten and fifteen.

If you hadn't become a writer, what would you have done? Continued reporting or become Wonder Woman.

Personally speaking . . .

What is the most daring or scary thing you've ever done? Ask a panel of editors if they were looking for a book like mine. Luckily, one said yes.

Describe your dream job? Writing books. My commute would be two seconds, my colleagues would be two sleeping pugs, and I could wear Yoga pants and a T-shirt.

What movie could you see over and over again? What book could you read over and over again? Am I a total nerd if I name two in each category? *Casablanca* and *Vertigo*. *Rain of Gold* by Victor Villaseñor and *Forever Amber* by Kathleen Winsor.

Favorite movie or TV villain? Alexis Morrell Carrington of *Dynasty*. They broke the mold when they made her.

Strangest gift you've ever received? A book about how to look like Marilyn Monroe. I still have it in case I ever write about a Marilyn impersonator.

What's next? I'm writing Isa's story! She's now divorced from the evil Carlos and raising her son. But one crazy night she and her son's sexy soccer coach get busy in the backseat of an SUV. Suddenly what was a one-night thing becomes something a little more permanent. ***SPOILER ALERT*** Susan plays heavily in the story. Tamara and Will make brief appearances—yes, they're still together and no, they're not married or pregnant yet.

Caras vemos,
corazones no sabemos

(You can't judge a book by its cover)

I started *Hot Tamara* in January 2002, after I'd been laid off and couldn't find another job if it fell on me. I went to the Latino Museum of Art in Long Beach for inspiration and while eating lunch at the restaurant next to the museum, I overheard my waitress tell her friends how her parents wouldn't let her attend a four-year university because they wanted her to get married and take care of them. Right then, Tamara was born. As I walked through the museum, the idea of Will emerged, and the next day when I sat down to flesh out my story, this cast of characters arrived with all of the complications they'd put in Tamara's life. The first day I sat down to write *Hot Tamara,* I wrote thirty pages, then went on to finish the first draft in six weeks.

I get asked a lot how I can sit in my office for hours on end making stuff up. The only viable reason, other than the fact that I'm antisocial, is that I come from a family of story-tellers. My mom makes a production of her stories, particularly of the night I was born when her ex-boyfriend from junior high gave her a tour of the hospital an hour before my arrival. On his days off, my dad—a firefighter of twenty-four years—would tell us of fires, car accidents, cliff rescues, and the occasional strange but true incidents where people lost their heads or jumped in front of the San Diego Trolley. And then there's my Grandma Margie, who will tell stories of my Great-great-great-grandmother Maria Duran, who survived the deaths of all of her children and moved with her two grandchildren from Anthony, New Mexico, to National City, California, where my family still lives.

Whereas my family tells stories on the phone, at dinner, or on road trips from Gila Bend, Arizona, I tell my stories on the page. Whereas their stories recount their own experiences, mine move far beyond my own life and into fiction. In many ways, *Hot Tamara* is a very personal story, and yet . . . isn't.

Writing *Hot Tamara* was a journey for me to realize how much of a Latina I really am. In my family we didn't speak Spanish or even identify ourselves as Mexican. I was a fourth-generation American on my dad's side, who happened to be Mexican. (*New Mexican* if you asked my Grandma Nana.) To my knowledge my mom has never made a tortilla, and for two Christmases she and my Auntie Betty made tamales, but since they don't drink, and they gossip all the time anyway, they didn't see the point of all that work.

When I started writing this book, to me it was about an American girl who happened to be Mexican and whose parents would speak broken Spanish in front of her when they didn't want her to know what they were saying. And I was satisfied with that story, until an agent took a look at it, and told me, "You need to make it more Latina."

I'd been hearing that all my life. Because of my coloring, people often think I'm Italian or Jewish. Then, after I say I'm Mexican American, they look so puzzled when they learn *I'm* not bilingual. Don't we all speak Spanish? Or, when they manage to pronounce my last name correctly, they insist my real first name is Maria not Mary. It was as if the Mexican part of my heritage was supposed to somehow negate the American part. As if I wasn't allowed to be both.

But if being "more Latina" would sell my book, then so be it. This was my dream, after all. In order to become more Latina, I bought *The Latina's Bible* by Sandra Guzman, *Latinas in Love* by Valerie Menard, and a subscription to *Latina* magazine.

I returned to my story, but even after sprinkling in some Spanish dialogue and explaining why Tamara serves her brother and father at the table, the book still wasn't Latina enough for that agent and several others.

I could have gone back again and tried to make Tamara and her family fit whatever mold these agents seemed to be looking for. I could have, but I didn't.

Before I found the editor who understood *Hot Tamara*'s cultural subtleties, I discovered there were so many women like me who were caught in that netherworld of "not being Latina enough." I learned that I don't need to look to others to justify my family and my heritage. Through this book, I feel a greater connection to Latinas and no longer feel the outsider. And I am even more proud to be among Latina writers bringing our unique experiences to readers. Perhaps *Hot Tamara* won't be required reading for American Lit, but for the woman reading it on her lunch break or on the train ride home, maybe she'll see some of herself and her family in the pages.

De tal palo, tal astila

(A chip off the old block)

Just in case you're wondering, Mary's mom, Celia Castillo (known as Marti to all), is nothing like Susan Contreras. To prove it, here is an unedited Q&A with Marti.

After you read the book, did you see yourself in the character of Susan (Tamara's mom)? No, in fact as soon as I finished the book, I yelled out loud, "It's not me!!"

How is Susan different from you? I would not choose what I want my child to be or do with her life. Children should be allowed to walk their own destiny.

What was your favorite scene? I could personally visualize the interactions between Tamara and Memo's scenes, especially when Susan disciplines them at the dinner table.

What was your least favorite scene? When Susan is verbally attacking Tamara's dreams.

Did you suspect that Mary might be writing family secrets in her book? No, not at all. Mary strives to be professional in all of her ventures. But she does have plenty of material for a great book . . .

What do you hope readers will take away after reading *Hot Tamara?* I hope that young girls will strive to live out their dreams and not be afraid to put themselves first!

What do you think is the most important part about being a mother? The most important part about being a mother is to listen before reacting.

The hardest part? The hardest part is when you have raised them and the house is empty.

Why do you think mother and daughter relationships can be so complicated? Mother and daughter relationships are complicated due to hormonal life stages. There are so many changes as we grow older, good and bad! But that is what life is all about!

Is it true that Mary really thought she was Wonder Woman and tied Frankenstein to a tree at the Tiny Tots Halloween party? Yes, she really did!! Over the PA system I heard, *"Would Wonder Woman's mother please come out to the courtyard. She has tied up Frankenstein to the palm tree!"* He was crying, and she stood there with her arms crossed. Mary still is Wonder Woman!

El bien no es conocido hasta que es perdido

(You don't know what you've got till it's gone)

They say that smells are the most powerful memory trigger, but for me it's music. I've always written to music, though I don't actually listen to the words while my characters are chatting away. The music sticks in my memory, and when I replay certain songs, parts of *Hot Tamara* immediately come back to life. I'm reminded not only of what the characters were doing, but of what I was feeling when I wrote the scenes as well.

With this in mind I've created a mini sound track for *Hot Tamara*. These are some of the most important songs that I played while writing, and a list of the scenes they correspond to. Listening to them as I read the book is, for me, an even better way to experience the story. Try it out.

1. "Amado Mio" (Pink Martini, Tortilla Soup)—Wedding rehearsal barbecue. This is one of those red-blooded, passionate *canciones del corazón* that always seemed to be playing on my grandmother's stereo when we visited. And it's a bit ironic given that Tamara is contemplating a new life while her mother tries to keep her under her thumb.

2. "Crash Into Me" (Dave Matthews Band, *Crash*)—When Will sees Tamara for the first time in nearly ten years, the longing and poignancy of this song captures that moment. Even though he's not yet completely in love with

her, part of him recognizes that she's someone he'll never forget. And likewise, so does Tamara.

3. "Saved The Best For Last" (Vanessa Williams)—This was my high school's prom song. I wasn't prom queen, and my date hated my dress. But I looked really good in that thing, and that's what mattered. Anyway, when Ruben gets down to propose, this song symbolizes all of the hopes he and Tamara had lost since they were the glittering prom king and queen in high school. And well, depending on how you look at it, Tamara really does save the best for last.

4. "Chicken Dance"—I don't know about you, but every Mexican wedding I've been to plays this song at one point during the reception. Come to think of it, every non-Mexican wedding I've been to plays this song, too. In either case, it's usually when everyone has had way too much to drink and they're falling over as they twist down before they clap clap clap.

5. "We Have Forgotten" (Sixpence None The Richer)— Now we're getting into spoiler territory, so I won't say much except that this song plays into the scene right after Memo gives Tamara her letter from USC.

6. "Perhaps, Perhaps, Perhaps" (Lila Downs)—Will and Kirsten. What can I say except who hasn't gone to school or even worked with a woman like Kirsten? While we can't stand them in real life, I understood and actually liked Kirsten. She's a girl who has been told her entire life that she's nothing without a man. Since Will fits her every ideal of one—after all he is on good behavior for Señora Allende's sake—she goes after him no holds barred.

7. "Just a Girl" (No Doubt)—This is an awesome song. If you really listen to it, Gwen's giving us girls a message

of empowerment, and it's particularly meaningful from a woman who's in a very machismo industry. So Gwen's I'm-fed-up-with-this-crap attitude is exactly what Tamara needs as she prepares to meet with Nadine Frazier.

8. "Moving On" (Sixpence None The Richer)—Again, spoiler territory. Listen to this song during chapter 10.

9. "Sunday Morning" (No Doubt)—Originally Isa had a major story line in the book that showed the end of her marriage. There was this great scene where she really kicked his cheating, Mama's boy butt. When Isa finally walks away from him, I imagine she's smiling, too.

10. *"La sitiera"* (Buena Vista Social Club Presents Omara Portuondo)—I love Omara Portuondo. Her voice is Ella Fitzgerald in that it transcends merely singing pretty words or making those funny dolphin squeals that Mariah Carey makes. Her voice comes from her soul, and her experiences give her an authority that most new singers don't yet have. Anyway, I always played her CD when I wrote Mrs. Allende's scenes. But this song in particular reminds me of the scene in chapter 14 where she and Will realize what it will mean when she's gone.

11. *Canciones de mi Padre*—Linda Ronstadt. I don't know why but it seems that every Mexican family has this CD and/or the second CD, *Mas Canciones*. So when Tamara comes home, this is what is playing on the stereo as it has been played at every barbecue, party, and bonfire. She realizes how isolated she's been without her family.

12. "El Farol" (Santana, Supernatural)—When Will and Tamara finally come together in chapter 21, it was one of those rare scenes that truly wrote itself. As a writer you live for those magical moments because so much of a book is unpeeling the layers and highlighting and honing

it until the images, emotions, and senses come to life. And this ballad fits the mood perfectly.

13. "Love" (Sixpence None The Richer)—Without giving anything away, chapter 25 is a major turning point in the book. This is where the fork in the road appears and at one time or another, we've all come to the point where we're faced with those life-changing decisions. Sometimes we know exactly what we're getting into, but this song is about the leap of faith we all take when we fall in love.

SPOILER ALERT

If you read this before the book, then get upset that I gave away the ending, you've been warned, so don't come crying to me.

14. "Kiss Me" (Sixpence None The Richer)—This song captures that giddy almost foolish feeling Tamara and Will have when they've realized they'll be together no matter what. I admit, I cried when I first wrote it and through all the drafts this book went through, this scene changed very little. Even though Tamara's decision is rather controversial to my way of thinking, it felt right that she did. If Will hadn't been willing to go wherever she goes and to stand behind her no matter what decision she made, then the story might've ended differently. So it's fitting in this case that alongside every great woman is a great man.

MARY CASTILLO has worked in public relations, advertising, and as a reporter for the *L.A. Times Community News*. A California native, Mary recently returned to her original love of storytelling. She is also the author of a short story; *Hot Tamara* is her first full-length novel.

MARY CASTILLO